I0627961

THE PROMISE OF AMERICA

& selected short stories

Helmut Stefan

BeachHouse Books

Saint Charles Missouri USA

THE PROMISE OF AMERICA &
selected short stories is Copyright 2015-2016 by
Helmut Stefan. all Rights reserved

Graphics Credits

Photos are from the author's private collection except for the photo of the Statue of Liberty, by Andrew Maiman, produced on 29 September, 2013. Mr Maiman graciously made this image available for common use by publishing with licensed under the Creative Commons Attribution-Share Alike 3.0 Unported license. the file was downloaded from the Wikimedia archives.

ISBN 978-1-59630-104-7

LCCN 2016954033

BeachHouse
Books

www.beachhousebooks.com

CONTENTS

Introduction 1

The Promise of America 3

The Violin 48

It's Not Going to Happen... 76

The Little Angel 83

Tick, tick, tick... 98

Call Me Hank 105

About the Author, Helmut Stefan 118

So, then, to every man his chance – to every man, regardless of his birth, his shining golden opportunity – to every man his right to live, to work, to be himself, to become whatever his manhood and his union can combine to make him – this, seeker, is the promise of America.

- Thomas Wolfe

INTRODUCTION

On the second Tuesday of every month, I go to a book club meeting at our local library. The reading group consists of about twelve or thirteen women and two men – I am one of these two men.

We read interesting books and our discussions are lively, stimulating and fun. I have learned so much from the books we have read and from our talks about them. After a particularly stirring discussion about a story which traced the history of a persecuted family, I made the statement that if we knew the life stories of the people around us, there would be no need to write fictional stories – these real life stories would be so fascinating and interesting as any one of the stories that was made up by a writer, no matter how skillful he or she was.

Some of the reading group members agreed with what I had said, but a few voiced their doubts – no, their life stories were not interesting, very humdrum, nothing extraordinary ever happened to them, etc.

And one of the ladies turned to me and said, "Maybe you said what you said because your life is interesting and exciting – you have been to so many places, and you came here as an immigrant.

So, why don't you tell us about your life? We are sure that you have an interesting story to tell."

To be sure, this was not what I had intended when I made my statement. As I sat there thinking what I should say, I noticed that there was absolute silence in the room and that all eyes were focused on me.

"Okay," I said, "if that's what you want, I'll give it a try, but..."

As I drove home from the meeting, there was just one thought that went through my mind over and over again, "When will you ever learn to keep your big mouth shut?"

THE PROMISE OF AMERICA

My story begins on the twelfth day of November 1942, in Neustettin, Germany, now Szczecinek, Poland. No, that's not right. I was born on the twelfth of November 1942, in Neustettin, Germany, now Szczecinek, Poland, all right, but that's not where my story begins. Every person's story begins long before he or she is born – and not only nine months before that – no, generations and generations before that. When we enter this world at our birth, we carry with us much more than just the inherited traits from our mother and father. We bring with us the experiences of our ancestors dating back many generations – in us there are the songs that they sang, the battles they fought, the languages they spoke, the food that they ate, the land they plowed, the forests in which they hunted and the gods that they worshiped. These generations of our ancestors are within us all and they have made us who we are today, just like our children and their children's children will have a tiny bit of us in them.

So now I must go back a few hundred years and speculate about how my ancestors wound up where they were. I know they were of German stock, but my parents had lived in Lithuania before

I was born. My brother Gustav, only five years older than myself, was born in Lithuania. Most likely they were part of the German settlers that were brought to this region when Frederick the Great of Prussia seized these lands. According to my father, our family had been there for generations (he didn't know either when they got there), but he knew that they were fully integrated into Lithuanian society. They attended Lithuanian school and spoke the language fluently. What made them different was the fact that they were Protestants, Lutherans, to be exact, while the Lithuanians are predominately Catholic, and for that reason they were always viewed somewhat as outsiders, and the locals called them "Prusei"_ - Prussians. My father and mother were married in Lithuania and, as already stated, my brother was born there. My family would have stayed there, but World War II broke out. My father was drafted into the German army and was sent to the Eastern Front. When the Russian troops began advancing from the East, the "German" families packed up their belongings and began the long and arduous trek toward the West. These convoys of oxcarts and horse-drawn wagons consisted mainly of women, children and old men. Thousands of them died of starvation, bombings and machine gun fire, or their carts broke through the ice of the lakes and rivers they had to cross and many of the people drowned. It was on this westward trek, in the middle of winter, that I was born. And now I will start my story again...

My mother was pregnant when she, her brother Georg (Jurgis – do you remember, The Jungle?), her sister Meta, her mother Martha and my brother Gustav began their westward journey. When they arrived in Neustettin, they stopped for a little while. It was here that I was born on November 12, 1942. I'm sure you won't forget this date after I have mentioned it now for the third time. Can you blame me? It was an important date in my life, wasn't it? My mother told me that a Polish woman gave her milk for her newborn baby. Without it, I would have died.

I don't know how long we stayed there, but the family had to move on. I never had a birth certificate – until a few years ago, when the American Social Security Administration, in order to verify my age (driver's license and naturalization papers were not good enough) wrote to the officials in Szczecinek to see whether there was a record of my birth. And lo and behold, a few months later, the Social Security Office sent me a beautiful, colorful certificate (in Polish) verifying that indeed there was a Helmut Stefan born in Szczecinek on that given date. Needless to say, I was absolutely amazed that this record still existed, keeping in mind that this was in the middle of the war when bullets were flying, bombs were falling all over the place and buildings and entire cities were going up in flames.

My mother had no idea where my father was during this time or whether he was even still alive. As it happened, my father was wounded – grenade splinters had seriously injured his right knee- and he was sent to Austria to recuperate.

My mother and her troop kept moving westward. When the war ended, they were in a refugee camp in the city of Lübeck, on the Baltic coast. By now, my father's wounds had healed well enough for him to be released from the hospital. That injury, he told us later, was the best thing that could have happened to him in the war. If he had stayed to fight, he would either have been killed or taken prisoner by the Russians. It turned out later that only a few German soldiers returned from the Russian prisoner of war camps. Most of them died in Siberia.

After my father had searched for weeks for his family, he was able, with the help of the International Red Cross, to locate his loved ones in the refugee camp in Bütow, near the Baltic Sea. There they stayed for several months until housing could be found for them and the thousands and thousands of other refugees who had fled to the West. Since many cities had been almost completely destroyed, most of the refugees were housed with farmers who were required to give up any additional space they had to quarter these displaced persons.

Our family was sent to Clues, a small farm village located about 20 miles south of Bremen, the next larger city. The village consisted of eight farmhouses. Our farmer's address was Clues No. 5. No street address needed. The farmhouse, built in 1849, was quite large. The front part housed some animals, cows and their calves. In the center part of this complex was a large open area. The cows faced in this direction. Above was a hayloft. During the winter months, when the cows were kept inside, all the farmer had to do was drop the straw and hay through a central opening to the space below, and then push it to the sides toward the cows and calves. Other animals were kept in adjoining buildings. The farmer never had to go outside during the winter to feed his livestock.

We – my father, mother, brother, grandmother and I – were assigned three small rooms on the second floor in the rear of the house. My brother and I slept in one room, my parents in another. My grandmother slept in the room that also served as a living room, kitchen and dining room. The toilet was outside. The stove was wood-fired and water had to be brought in from the well outside the house.

Our bedrooms were not heated. When my brother and I ran our fingers along the slanted roof, which was inches above our heads, we would have frost under our fingernails. Our mattresses and comforters, stuffed with straw, kept us fairly warm at night.

My first real memories of my life at that time go back to my years at school. It was customary for children to begin first grade at the age of six; there was no kindergarten. The school itself had two classrooms. Students in grades one through four were taught in one classroom. Students in grades five through eight, in another. We sat on benches along a fairly long desk, always four in a row. Each desk had four holes in it to hold the inkbottles, which were used in the higher grades. The school was in the next larger town, Heiligenfelde, and was a little more than a mile from our house. The children from the surrounding farm villages came here, too. At first, my brother and I walked to school, but when I was a little older, we rode our bicycles.

In the spring and fall, our school hours were from 7:00 a.m. to 11:00 a.m. In the winter, the hours were from 8:00 a.m. to 12 noon. There were two recesses in the school day. The first came after about an hour of instruction; the second one after another hour of instruction. There were no bells. The two teachers decided when the recesses would happen. When the weather was nice, we went outside. Our teachers, Herr Wolters and Herr Stobbe, would walk back and forth across the schoolyard, each smoking his cigar or pipe. (Our parents did not complain about our teachers smoking openly in front of us.)

When it snowed, we were told to bring our sleds to school. We would walk to a hill not too far from the school and spend all morning sledding. We would then be allowed to go home. This happened several times each winter.

Another day that we always looked forward to was the day when a station wagon would pull up in front of the school and a man carried in an old-fashioned reel-to-reel movie projector. This would mean that the morning would be spent watching a movie. These were usually movies that took us to distant places like Alaska, the Sahara Desert, the Amazon Rain Forest or other far away exotic places. Most of us had never been further than twenty miles from our little village. We would sit in utter amazement, fascinated by the fact that places like this existed on this earth.

On our way to school, we would have to pass the town's church. It was old, very old, but I don't know when it was built. The church steeple, which was at most as high as a five-story building, seemed to be reaching right up into the sky. I often wondered how the workmen had been able to put the gray tiles up so high on the steep spire and attach a huge metal cross all the way on top.

My mother would take me to Bremen once a year to buy me shoes. This was always an exciting adventure because it meant an hour bus ride with all the sights that were to be seen along the way. Actually, there wasn't that much to see: potato and sugar beet fields and rye and wheat fields. The small towns that we drove through had nothing very interesting to show, and yet, I was fascinated to be moving along at thirty miles an hour. What a thrill! After we had bought my shoes and a few other things that my mother needed, we would go to the bus stop for our ride back home. This was near the train station. Now came the best part of all. There was a fruit stand right next to the bus stop and this fruit vendor actually had bananas for sale. My mother would buy one for me. I would eat it on my way home. I ate it so slowly savoring each tiny bite so much, that usually I finished it just before we got home. That was one of the great treats of my childhood.

I began confirmation class instruction every Saturday morning when I was twelve years old. On my way home after class, my friends and I would stop at the local inn for an even more special treat – ice cream. My mother had given me ten pfennigs along just for this purpose. During the summer months, the innkeeper sold ice cream, along with the usual more adult refreshments. For the above-mentioned ten pfennigs, he would carefully place a ping-pong ball sized scoop of ice cream on a shell-shaped wafer. Vanilla only. No other flavors were offered. Again, I savored my scoop for as long as I could. What a delicacy! And this was only during the summer months – after all, who ever heard of anyone eating ice cream when it was cold outside?

My mother or grandmother (mother often worked in the fields) would, once in a while, have a special treat for me when I came home from school. This would be a slice of fried bread and a fried egg. Yes, a fried egg was an absolute delicacy.

I could not imagine a better gift for my birthday than a chocolate bar from each of my friends. This was the usual gift for a child's birthday. For every one of us, to have three or four chocolate bars, which would be slowly devoured in the course of several week or months – well, nothing could be more wonderful!

Not far from the farm were several good-sized stretches of forests, a small river and several little ponds. We would go hunting for mushrooms in the fall. We knew exactly where the mushrooms could be found. We knew which ones were edible and which ones were poisonous. One thing we did not know was that one kind of mushroom, which we found in great abundance, was actually considered to be quite a delicacy. These were the chanterelles. They were often covered by dry grass and not easily visible. Since we, however, were smart enough to cut them – never pull them out of the ground – they would always grow back after a rain in just a few days. We would go and harvest them again and again. Our mothers fried these mushrooms along with green onions and served them with boiled potatoes – a very inexpensive meal for our family. Later, in Chicago, I learned that just a few ounces of these mushrooms cost more than I would care to pay for them now.

The games we played were simple games and we made our own toys. Playing cowboys and Indians was the "in" thing. If we saw a tree branch that had a nice straight part with a proper curvature to it (the handle), we would cut it off the tree and make something out of it, which kind of resembled a gun. That was good enough for us. We did a much better job with bows and arrows. It was common knowledge that a nice straight branch from a hazelnut tree made the best bow and the arrows were made from reeds from our ponds. We never shot anything with these fierce weapons. Just making them and then testing them, by shooting at a nearby tree, was super fun for us. We actually knew nothing about real cowboys and Indians, except what we saw in the Western films, which were so popular at the time.

One of the great benefits of growing up in the country was that all around us there were wonderful things to eat – all we had to do was to pick them up. Apple, pear and plum orchards surrounded each farmer's house. We knew which tree at which farm had the most delicious apples at any given time. The same was true for the pears and plums. We never picked these fruits from the trees – that would have been stealing. But if they had fallen to the ground, we were allowed to pick them up and eat all we wanted. The greatest fun came during the cherry-picking season. That is when we boys were actually asked to help pick the cherries (the men were busy in the fields) and we did work very hard, and it was quite all right for us to eat all the cherries we wanted.

Each farmer had a vegetable garden behind the house. Here they grew beans, peas, carrots, asparagus and spinach. There were rows and rows of strawberries, raspberries, gooseberries and red and black currants. We always had our fill and suffered stomachaches quite frequently, because we often ate all of these fruits before they were really ripe.

There were plenty of wild raspberries and blackberries along the country lanes. Usually these grew among the stinging nettles. These made our skins turn a blotchy red wherever they touched us. This, however, did not stop us from enjoying them. Those berries looked so inviting and we had to have them.

The greatest and most plentiful treats were the blueberries. They grew in great abundance in all of the woods in our area. We picked these by the buckets and brought them home. We ate them with either cold water or milk, with pieces of bread crumbled into the bowl and sprinkled with sugar – absolutely delicious and refreshing!

When everything had been harvested in the fall, we would visit the potato fields once again. There were always a few more potatoes to be found. We would make a fire into which we threw the potatoes. Once only ashes were left, we would pull out our potatoes, carefully peel away the blackened outer skin and eat perfectly done baked potatoes. Of course, our hands and our faces were also black by the time we finished our al fresco meal.

One silly thing that sticks in my mind, of all the crazy things we did as kids, was the semi-annual dunk contest. This is how it went. My two friends, Heiner and Peter, and I had an ongoing contest with kids from the neighboring towns – who would be the first and the last to completely dunk themself in the nearby pond known as the clay pit. Early in the spring – the ice had barely melted – the three of us would go to the pond, strip down butt-naked, wade belly deep into the water and quickly submerge ourselves completely in the water. That was the stipulation. You had to be totally wet. This was always done in complete secrecy. We could not tell our mothers that we wanted our swimming trunks; our mothers would have never permitted this. The same thing happened in the late fall. Sometimes there was already the slightest layer of ice on the water, but we had to do it. This was a point of honor – bragging rights. That we could have gotten seriously ill at these silly escapades never entered our minds.

Life was simple and good, at least that's the way it seemed to us kids. We had tremendous freedom. We chopped down fairly good-sized trees and built tepees. We would make rafts to navigate the ponds. We fished in the ponds with our homemade fishing poles. We were in close touch with nature. I remember the blossoming pussy willow trees; yes, trees! They were bright yellow and there were thousands of honeybees in them. One of the most beautiful sights were the young birch trees in spring when the first buds of the fragile green appeared. They were so graceful, always swaying with the wind. The meadows were filled with bright dandelions. Nobody considered them to be a weed, not even the farmers, because they knew that when the cows ate them, they produced better milk.

It was our job to find a Christmas tree. All year long, my friends and I were on the lookout for that perfect tree. Once we had each claimed our tree, it was understood that no one else would cut down that tree. We would chop down "our" tree the day before Christmas Eve and bring it home. Of course, what we did was illegal, but no one cared, there were so many trees all around us. The tree was decorated with tinsel, walnuts and pinecones that had been painted silver or gold. Best of all, however, were the candles – real candles, always white – that were stuck into metal holders, which clipped onto the branches. The tree was only lit on Christmas Eve and on the night of Christmas Day. The lights were turned off and the candles gave off a glittering light that was just magical. When the burning candles touched the needles of the branch above, there was a wonderful pine aroma that filled the room. There were not many presents under the tree, but with us singing "Stille Nacht heilige Nacht," up in our living room/dining room/kitchen, there was an indelible image of a happy family, a memory that has remained with me until today.

A few years before my retirement, one of my colleagues asked if I knew what gleaners were. She had seen the famous painting, "The Gleaners" by Jean-Francois Millet. When she looked at the picture, she had not really understood the title. I told her that not only did I know what gleaners were, but also that I had been a gleaner. When the harvest is complete, the landowners allowed the peasants to go over the fields and gather everything that they could still find. That's what our farmers did, too. We, the refugees, were allowed to go out into the fields and collect anything that was still left behind. After our entire family spent several hours on a potato field, we might have found a hundred pounds of potatoes. That would last us through most of the winter. With other food items gradually becoming more available, we did not starve.

When I look back on my childhood, I'm amazed to find that I never realized how poor my family was. My parents worked at any job they could get. When there was no work in our area, my father traveled to the Rhineland to work in a pumice stone mine. He would be gone for weeks, but my mother would receive a few marks for the household. My mother helped out on the farm, but on the side she worked as a seamstress. Since in those days everything had to be mended and passed on from the older child to the younger one, there was a real demand for her talent. Even my brother and I helped out by steering the horses during the harvest. The men were busy pitching the hay or bundles of wheat or rye onto the wagons where the women and girls stacked them in neat rows until the grain was piled high above the side rails of the wagon. By letting us boys drive the horses, no valuable time was lost by having to stop at each stack of grain. The farmer would then give us a few marks, too, and all of us would be invited to eat supper with the farmer and his regular farmhands.

Yes, we were poor, very poor, and yet I feel that I had the most wonderful childhood any child could ever have. In our little country school, I learned to love music. Herr Wolters had started a choir consisting of students from the fifth to the eighth grade. The group was made up of 25 singers, all carefully chosen by the teacher and I was one of them. There, in that little old schoolhouse, we sang songs in two and three-part harmony often accompanied by Herr Wolters on the piano. I learned later that our teacher was quite famous as a pianist and organist. He gave performances on Sundays in Bremen that were broadcast on the radio. Our group sang as well and definitely better than any elementary school group I have ever heard.

There was always music in our house when my mother's brother Onkel Georg and her sister Tante Meta came to visit. They both played the bandonika, a small button accordion, to which they sang in perfect harmony. We would sing along with them and we knew the words by heart.

It was during my childhood that I learned to appreciate the beauty of nature. I enjoyed walking through the dense pine forest – so still and so fragrant. Birch trees are still my favorite and they grew well in our region. The first gentle green buds

17

on the slender white branches were a clear sign that spring was on its way. We ate fresh fruits and vegetables and drank the clear water that sprang from underneath a rock in the quiet forest and then bubbled along to join the slightly larger brook about a mile away. We children were allowed to be children. We had more freedom to do anything we wanted to do than any child in a city could ever have. We were not aware of any violence or any sort of crime. Every year we looked forward to when the Marksman's Club would have their annual festival. Then there would be a carousel set up for the kids and the adults would dance in the tent until the morning hours.

The greatest gift, however, that I took with me from those days is that I had learned to appreciate every good thing that had happened to me then, and even more so in the life that still lay ahead of me.

I must have been ten or eleven when I first heard my parents talk about the possibility of us emigrating to the United States of America. Letters had been exchanged with distant relatives on my mother's side. They had moved to Chicago in the late forties and they wrote to my parents, that although the streets in America were not paved with gold, there was plenty of work. In this post-war time, the factories were running at full capacity and back then, Chicago was a manufacturing city. Large and small companies were begging for workers. The fact that most of these newcomers did not know the language was not a problem. Someone could always be found to explain the work to the new arrivals and they learned quickly.

One day my father announced that we would be going to Hamburg. This is where the American Embassy was located. Papers had already been filled out and submitted and now we had to go for an interview. We arrived in Hamburg after we had taken the local train to Bremen and from here the much faster inter-city train to Hamburg. The train ride itself was the most fascinating part of the trip for me.

The American Embassy was located in a beautiful white villa along the Alster River. This had been, and now is once again, the most fashionable part of Hamburg. Back then the city was in the process of being rebuilt. Since Hamburg was the most important German port city, it had been almost completely leveled during the war. I don't remember seeing much of the city, but I do remember the white building. I had the good fortune of going there not that many years ago when I was one of the teachers who accompanied Chicago German language students on their exchange program with the city of Hamburg, a sister city of Chicago. The American ambassador had invited the group to visit. I told him and our students that my family's journey to a new life in American had begun right here, in this white building on the beautiful Alster River.

I don't remember the interview at all. I am sure that the American authorities wanted to see the actual prospective immigrants in person and determine whether they were physically and mentally the kind of people that would fit into American society. There was also the question with German men whether they had been active Nazis. This was not a problem for my father. Where he had lived as a young man there had not been a Hitler Youth or even an organized Nazi Party. He was drafted into the army when the war was already well under way. He reached the rank of corporal during his military service. He was wounded and sent to Austria to recuperate. The fact that we were given permission to emigrate showed that the Americans had found nothing objectionable in my father's background.

It seemed that we were all set to go, but that was not the case. My brother became sick – osteomyelitis – a serious bone disease that most often affects children and teenagers. He was hospitalized on and off for several months. The hospital where he was treated seemed primitive by today's standards. I am sure that the proper medication was not available. He was finally well enough for my parents to try again to go to America. We were off to Hamburg again, to that same white mansion. We received another approval two years after our first attempt and now we were definitely all set to go.

We arrived in Bremerhaven on May 12, 1956, ready for departure. All we had were our suitcases in our hands. A larger wooden crate, which had been made by our local carpenter, had already been shipped. We were housed in a long barrack-like building in Bremerhaven along with hundreds of other waiting immigrants. Each of us had to wear a wide ribbon around our necks to which were attached several large plastic cards. This made us look like today's VIP's at sporting and entertainment events. We stayed here for three days. I remember that we were fed quite well; orange juice, toast and scrambled eggs with sausages for breakfast. That was mind-blowing! Who eats fried sausages for breakfast?

On the second day in the camp, my father met an old army buddy who had been in the same unit with him on the Eastern Front. They had a lot to tell each other about their lives since the end of the war. It turned out that this family – husband, wife and four children – were also going to Chicago. We exchanged addresses. We later learned that they went to the Marquette Park area while my family was headed to Brighton Park. To visit with each other all we had to do was catch the Kedzie Avenue bus. Small world, indeed!

We were taken by bus on May 15, 1956, to our ship, the USS General Langfitt. This was a United States Army troop transport ship. The males were quartered in one part of the ship and the females and small children in another. Families were able to reunite during the day and have their meals together.

We were told to report to the deck of the ship after we had stowed away our luggage. Quite a few people had gathered on the dock and as the ship pulled away, a brass band played on the pier, "Nun ade, du mein lieb' Heimatland, lieb' Heimatland, ade." (Now farewell, my dear fatherland, dear fatherland, farewell.) Handkerchiefs were waved on the land as well as on the ship. I am sure that many of them dabbed a reddened, tearful eye.

I have often thought back to our leaving the old country and I am amazed at my lack of emotions at this life-changing event. Yes, I was sad to leave my friends, our village and the woods. Life had been good; at least that is how I saw it, through my childish eyes. I had not suffered want; I had always been safe (I had never heard of any crime being committed anywhere). I liked the school that I attended. But even at that age, I had my concerns. What would life be like in a strange country so far away? How would I get along in school not knowing English? Would I make any friends? These thoughts were in the back of my mind, but they did not overwhelm me. Just once in a while, I would experience a queasy feeling in my stomach and I would ask myself, "What am I getting into? Will I be able to make it?"

All of these very legitimate concerns were overshadowed by a sense of excitement and adventure. Going to America! What could be greater than that? This was the land of cowboys and Indians, the land of endless highways, of gangsters and immigrants from every corner of the world. Even in our little town, I had heard on our Grundig radio Bill Haley and the Comets sing,

"Rock Around the Clock." That was so crazy and wild. I didn't know there could be music like this. We were going to the land of opportunity. I would have gone one more year to elementary school in Germany and then I would have become an apprentice. For refugee kids like us, it was impossible to go on to any kind of higher education. To go on to the Mittelschule (if accepted) meant a daily bus ride to the next larger town called Syke. It would have also required better clothing and the purchase of school supplies. Money my parents did not have. This was simply not possible. Since I was rather small for my age, I might have been apprenticed to become a tailor or salesman. I don't think I would have been accepted as an apprentice to become a bricklayer, carpenter, mechanic or any profession that required a certain degree of physical strength. So, America lay before me and I went along gladly, for even that little fellow that I was, I had some confidence in myself. I was inquisitive, eager to see what lay ahead. I had seen quite a few Westerns, drank Coca Cola and enjoyed Wrigley's chewing gum – all wonderful American things. Now we just had to cross that big, deep ocean for the adventure to begin.

The USS General Langfitt was an 18,000-ton troop transport ship. This was very small compared to today's cruise ships. We did not sleep in cabins, but rather in hammocks, suspended from the ceiling, four on top of one another. The top one was left unoccupied, but the people sleeping in the lowest and second lowest hammock had the one above him about five inches from his face. The toilets and showers were all open – no walls or curtains. This was very strange to me.

'etzter Gruß aus Bremen vor der Überfahrt   „General Langfitt"

Nun ade, du mein lieb' Heimatland

Laß die Winde stürmen
    auf des Lebens Bahn;
ob sich die Wogen türmen
    gegen deinen Kahn,
segle ruhig weiter,
    wenn der Mast auch bricht,
Gott ist dein Begleiter,
    er vergißt dich nicht!

1. Nun ade, du mein lieb' Heimatland, lieb' Heimatland, ade! Es geht jetzt fort zum fernen Strand, lieb' Heimatland, ade! Und so sing' ich denn mit frohem Mut, wie man singet, wenn man wandern tut, lieb' Heimatland, ade!
2. Wie du lachst mit deines Himmels Blau, lieb' Heimatland, ade! Wie du grüßest mich mit Feld und Au, lieb' Heimatland, ade! Gott weiß, zu dir steht stets mein Sinn, doch jetzt zieht's mich zur Ferne hin, lieb' Heimatland, ade!
3. Begleitest mich, du lieber Fluß, lieb' Heimatland, ade! Bist traurig, daß ich wandern muß, lieb' Heimatland, ade! Vom moos gen Stein am wald'gen Tal, da grüß ich dich zum letztenmal Heimatland, ade!

Food was served in the mess hall – cafeteria-style. We walked along with our trays and the men behind the counters gave us a helping of whatever we pointed to. You were even allowed to go back for seconds. I had never seen this much food in one place before. Most of it tasted pretty good, some of it was a little strange and some was just very unpleasant. The weirdest taste of all was that of grapefruit juice. My father said it reminded him of the smell you got when you scraped a horse's foot in preparation for putting on a new horseshoe. I found the taste quite repulsive! This juice was served from huge cans and I'm sure it tasted nothing like the freshly squeezed juice we drink today. Fried potatoes – for breakfast? Strange, these American customs, but absolutely fascinating!

All adults had to help to keep the ship clean. The leftovers and other refuse were collected in huge cans and the contents dumped overboard – that was obviously the reason why the ship was always followed by a group of dolphins. Everyone was kept busy sweeping up or carrying supplies from one place to another, but no one complained. This was easy work in comparison to what they had to do before. I learned later that this voyage was not free. My parents sent a small sum of money to the government at the beginning of every month. I don't know how much this transport cost for us – by today's standards it was probably a laughable amount, but to the immigrants, it was a very serious matter. These people were not used to owing money.

The journey started out quite well. The weather was beautiful and most people were on deck. I sat on a bench on the starboard side and watched the waves roll by as we headed into the North Sea. I had to chuckle to myself – some people had talked about seasickness. That was ridiculous! Gliding through the water like this was wonderful; I certainly would not get sick. Some time later, an announcement was made to look out to the landside. There we could see the white cliffs of Dover. I knew that France was on the other side and soon we would leave Europe behind us. As I looked out to sea, which was just a few feet below my feet, I noticed that the color of the water began to change. The friendly green color was becoming darker and soon it was all black. The motion of the ship began to change, too. Up to now, the ship had basically rolled gently from side to side, but now the front part began to dip down into the water with the rear rising up. Then, the front would move up and the rear sank down into the sea. As I stood there and watched this happening, I began to notice a funny feeling in my stomach. This turned from a slight discomfort into real nausea. It didn't take long before I was grasping the railing and emptied the contents of my stomach into the sea. There was no doubt about it – we were now in the Atlantic Ocean. I spent the next two days in my hammock, either sleeping or vomiting. I ate very little – everything came up right away, anyway. By the third day, I was well enough to go back on deck and to eat a little something. After this experience, the journey was quite pleasant. The American sailors were very nice to us. They must have found us as foreign as we found them. This is the first time that I saw black men go about their work just like the other men. They walked and talked and laughed just like the others. That was, of course, not surprising, it's just that we had never thought about black people as just being like other people. We had only seen pictures of them in our geography book and we had seen them dance in their African clay hut villages. Every day there was a new discovery to be made.

After nine days at sea, we were told that on the next morning we were to assemble on deck at five o'clock in the morning. The ship had anchored just outside of New York harbor. Now in the early morning mist the ship began to slowly move toward land – the land that would be our new homeland. The date was May 25, 1956.

Suddenly, out of the mist, we saw the Statue of Liberty, as the Star-Spangled Banner sounded from the loudspeakers. We all realized that this was a very special moment in our lives, but I am sure that most of the adults said a silent prayer asking for help and guidance for this new phase in everyone's life.

The ship sailed on slowly and soon we saw the Manhattan skyline rise before us. Even though it is not the same skyline today, many of the great buildings had already been built, such as the

Chrysler Building and the Empire State Building. These and other buildings stood looking like great fingers pointing to the heavens. This was an overwhelming sight to behold and for someone like me, who had never seen anything taller than the cathedral in Bremen, this view made an impression on me; an impression I would never forget. We were in America and all we could do was to wait and see what would happen next.

The ship pulled along a pier and we walked down the gangplank into our new lives. We were led into a huge hangar-like building. Here we saw endless boxes and crates and barrels. We kept walking, with our tags around our necks, like sheep that would go anywhere they were told to go. But then I asked my parents to stop for just a minute. My stomach began turning again and without warning I began to puke again, even more violently than I had done on the ship. I'm sure there was more food in my stomach. I have been told this is not an uncommon occurrence – when the swaying of the ship stops, people begin to feel sick again. Whenever I told my students about my arrival in America, I always embellished the story. "You have probably seen the footage of Pope John Paul II arriving in some foreign country. When he steps from the plane, he always kisses the ground of the country he is visiting. Well, my greeting to America was not quite as elegant and touching as his – I stood hunched over the boxes and crates and emptied my stomach on the soil of my new homeland." My students made me tell that story time and time again.

A bus took us to the train station where we boarded the train for Chicago. I don't remember anything about the bus ride through New York City. The train ride to Chicago took two days, but I cannot recall anything specific about it except that it seemed to me that we rode on and on forever, and my knowledge of geography was good enough to know that when we reached Chicago, we would not even have traveled halfway through this huge country.

Our host was waiting for us at Dearborn Station. The husband had come alone so that we would all fit into his car. Once our luggage was stored away in the huge trunk - I now believe it was a 1949 Oldsmobile, with those huge chromed "teeth" that made up the grille - we got into the car for the ride to our new home. We had never been inside a car like this before. Everything about it was big and heavy. The suspension was so soft that one felt one was riding on butter. The ride seemed endless - street after street after street. How large could this city possibly be?

After a touching reunion between our hosts and my parents, we all sat down and partook of the feast that the lady of the house had prepared for us. The table was laden with the most delicious looking delicacies - a bowl full of Polish sausage, fried chicken and pork chops. There was a huge plate filled with thick yellow and buttery pieces of kugelis - a delicious Lithuanian potato concoction.

This version had bits of smoked ham in it. There were several bowls filled with vegetables. I was familiar with peas, beans and carrots, but there was another one, yellow in color, which I had never seen before. This was corn, we were told, and I liked it immediately!

Our host family had prepared a small apartment for us on the first floor. There were two bedrooms and a kitchen and a large empty room, which had once served as a store. This is where we stored everything we had, including the wooden crate, which arrived about a week later. The place was small, but we had a refrigerator, a television set, and a gas range. Plates and cups and silverware were already neatly stored away in the drawers and cupboards. Hot and cold running water was available at the turn of a faucet. There was a bathroom, complete with a flush toilet and a bathtub with a shower in it. The place was small, but for now it was more than sufficient.

We arrived in Chicago on a Saturday. The next morning, after breakfast, we walked around the neighborhood to familiarize ourselves with our new environment. The area wasn't pretty, but down the side streets, just off Kedzie Avenue, there were nice two flat houses with a little grass here and there. However, flowers seemed to be an unknown commodity in this part of the city.

The host family once again provided us with a sumptuous feast at lunchtime. So much food and everything was so delicious. The men drank beer, Nectar beer, to be exact, which our host poured from quart bottles into huge glasses. The women and children drank soda. The host family had two boys; ages five and eleven. The older boy kept us supplied with strawberry, raspberry, orange and cream soda, as well as ginger ale. This was something we had never tasted before. There were several wooden crates on the back porch. Each crate was filled with twelve one-quart bottles of this delicious liquid. These beverages were made by the Burckhardt Company located somewhere around 18th and Halsted Streets. I know this because sometimes I drove along with the father to pick up several cases of this colorful soda. I'm sure that it did not consist of much more than water, artificial flavoring, artificial color and sugar. All of this did not matter much to us.

Later that afternoon, the pastor, who had been instrumental in getting us to come to America, came to visit us. The Lutheran Church Missouri Synod was involved in bringing a large number of Lutheran German refugees to this country. Other religious denominations were doing the same thing. This pastor told us that he had already found work for my father and my brother, who was now nineteen years old. A tool and die shop, on 26th Street right across from the Cook County Jail, owned by two Germans had agreed to hire both of them, sight unseen. This was great news and my parents and brother thanked him profusely – no one asked what the salary would be.

I did not go to school right away because summer vacation was just two or three weeks away. I would register during the summer and then begin with the fall semester.

Our most pleasant surprise during our early stay in America occurred on the following Friday. As was the custom back then, my father and my brother received their first week's pay in cash in their pay envelopes. Their combined pay was less than a hundred dollars. August, the host father, drove the four of us to the nearest supermarket, a Del Farm store. We had never been in a store like that. We took a shopping cart (just like the other people) and began to move down the aisles. My mother could not believe what she saw. In the produce section were fruits and vegetables piled high. One table was filled with just bananas, another with oranges. There were strawberries, blueberries, lemons, limes, coconuts and pineapples. There before us lay every vegetable that we were familiar with and many that we did not know. The biggest thrill came when we arrived at the meat counter. Here were thick steaks, juicy pork chops, ground beef and pork, tongue and liver and pork hocks and row after row of sausages and cold cuts. My mother watched with astonishment as the people around us were taking package after package of different kinds of meat and placing them into their carts. They did it so naturally as if there were nothing to it, as if this was the way it was supposed to be. I remember that my mother had tears in her eyes. All of this could be hers, too. We had more than enough money to buy anything she wanted. Milk by the gallon – unheard of! Coffee in two-pound cans – was it really possible that one could buy so much at a time? I know that my mother considered every purchase carefully. The idea to buy food for a week or two in advance was something totally new to her. She did not buy a steak for each of us. One of these steaks properly prepared in a stew or as a goulash, would feed the entire family. But she did buy bananas and flour and sugar, bread and jam and everything else that she thought she needed. We laughed as we carried the grocery bags into the house and watching her place everything into the refrigerator or the various cupboards was almost a religious experience.

I spent the summer getting used to the American ways. The two host family sons showed me games they played. It seemed very strange that two people could enjoy throwing a ball back and forth and catching it with a big, leather glove on one hand. They could do this for hours on end. Then, you would have to hit this ball with a stick. Since they used a much bigger ball for this, I was able to hit the ball once in a while. Sometimes they would bring out another kind of ball – a funny-shaped oblong ball that was difficult to catch and even harder to throw. These games were played in a vacant lot where there were bricks lying around and also broken glass. No trees anywhere.

Of course, we also had to get new clothing for our new environment. We were told that I definitely needed jeans, so my mother and I bought a pair at the Archer Avenue Big Store. Since these pants were much too long for me, my mother shortened them so that they were just the right length. This, we were told, was the wrong thing to do. The proper thing to do was to simply roll them up. That was cool! We had to buy another pair of jeans.

I also needed new shoes, summer shoes. We went back to the store to buy a pair of sneakers, the low kind that I used to wear back home. This again was a mistake. My new friends told me that only girls wore these types of shoes; boys always wore high tops. Back to the store we went.

At the end of August, my host mother took my mother and me to register for school – Davis Elementary School at Pershing and Albany. This was a tall, dark and imposing structure. The gym alone was larger than the two classrooms of our little country school combined. The registration went well and I was told to report at nine o'clock on the Tuesday after Labor Day in September.

The summer was over – and it had been a hot summer. We did not have air-conditioning. Opening the windows did not help either because the houses on both sides of ours were no more than five feet away. There was no breeze.

We had become quite used to our new life during these first months in our new country. We had plenty to eat and we ate well. I gained at least twenty pounds during the last few months. My mother, father and brother also looked stronger with more color in their cheeks. Shopping was still a great experience for my mother. She could basically buy anything she wanted. Just a few months ago she bought an egg or two at a time – here they came by the dozen. A quart of milk had been a luxury – here the milk came by the gallon. Since my mother was a seamstress, she made many of her own dresses. I remember seeing her at the store, picking up bolt after bolt of material. All she had to do was decide what color or pattern she wanted – she could have it. My father and brother were happy with their jobs, too. They each got their pay envelopes every Friday and they couldn't believe all the things they could buy with that money. We got a window unit air-conditioner. My mother got new pots and pans. The adults drank real coffee and not that "ersatz" mixture that had very little resemblance to real coffee.

One Sunday afternoon, after we had eaten lunch with our host family, the lady asked me if I would like some ice cream. Of course, I did. I could not believe my eyes when she pulled out a box filled with wafer ice cream cones. She took a half-gallon carton of ice cream from the freezer and filled the cone with ice cream and planted another huge ball of that delicious cold delicacy on top of it. I thanked her and began to eat this total treat. When I saw her just a little while later, she asked me if I liked the ice cream and if I would like another one. I couldn't believe my ears. It was then long before I ever heard it from that Russian comedian, that I said to myself, "America, what a country!"

We drove out into the country almost every weekend and had a picnic. There were baskets filled with fried chicken, sausages, potato salad, pickles and who knows what else. There was always a cooler along with cold drinks – Burckhardt soda for the kids and Nectar beer for the adults. Although it had seemed that we had driven way out into the country for our weekend picnics, I realized much later that we had actually only been as far as Maple Lake. But that was all right. Everything was new, fresh, bountiful and wonderful.

Labor Day came soon enough and now life became more serious for me, too. I had to go to school. Davis Elementary was four blocks from our house and I had no problem walking there in the morning and back in the afternoon.

My first day at school was pleasant enough. I was placed into a 7th grade classroom. The teacher was very nice and introduced me to my new classmates. Most of them nodded a friendly hello to me, but I could see that amazement in their eyes. A new kid, and from Germany no less – this was just eleven years after World War II had ended. I was assigned a seat toward the back of the room. I had my own seat. There were no benches here. As I looked around the room, I noticed one thing about the other kids right away – they were so big! To be sure, I knew that I was small for my age, but these kids – and especially the girls – some looked like adult women to me. I sat and listened and understood nothing. After an hour, I experienced my first surprise about the American school system. Two older students pushed a cart into the room and began handing out cookies – you only had to tell them how many you wanted. The other student passed out bottles of milk – white or chocolate – your pick. I pointed to the white milk and took one cookie. We all sat there and ate our morning snack. I couldn't believe this – milk and cookies served in the classroom. Again, I beat the Russian comedian to the punch and said to myself, "America, what a country!" I found out later that students paid two cents for the milk and one cent for each cookie. From then on I brought a nickel to school with me each day – one milk and three cookies – I gained more weight!

After two days in the seventh grade classroom, I was taken downstairs and put in a room of second graders. I was given the same books as they had and followed along with the lessons. Once in a while the teacher would check with me to see whether I understood what was going on. I usually had no problem. The first thing I learned was that in English you write one thing, and you say another. There are also so many silent letters. The "w" is not pronounced at all, etc., etc. In order to get the spelling right, I pronounced the words phonetically in my head. An example: suitcase – in my mind, I would say – "sue – it – ka – ze." The letter "a" is a major problem for any foreigner who is learning English. In the alphabet you say, a, b, c. But then we took the bus that went down Archer

Avenue. Words like awkward, attention, April and others, all require special consideration.

I stayed in the second grade for about a month. Then I was returned to be with the seventh graders. There was no bilingual teacher. There was no one who spoke my language. Everyone was kind and helpful, and when I returned to my proper group, I was able to function on my own. As a matter of fact, I was soon the best speller in the class – not because I'm so bright, but because I used my phonetic system in which every letter is pronounced. We had to learn ten new words every week and I got a 100% on every spelling test.

School in Chicago was quite different than what I was accustomed to. First of all, the building itself was impressive. There were three floors of long corridors, a huge gym, a large lunchroom and toilets on every floor for the students and teachers.

The behavior in the classroom was something that stunned me. The first time I saw a student get up, walk to the waste paper basket, throw in a piece of paper and then casually return to his seat, I wondered what was going to happen now. Well, nothing happened. So, a student could just get up and walk around whenever he or she felt like it? Impossible! It also amazed me that students could just yell out answers without raising their hands. To be sure, at times the teacher would ask them to do so, but it didn't help very much. One day, a student got into a shouting match with the teacher. He called her dirty names (even I could understand that) and went on and on about how she was a bad teacher and how stupid she was, and how he wished that she would just drop dead. I sat there in shock. What would happen now? The teacher asked him to go to the office. We did not see him for the rest of the day, but the next day he was back in the classroom as if nothing had happened.

Other things were different, too. It surprised me to see that all written work was done on lined sheets of paper that were ripped out of a notebook, frayed edges and all, when the work had to be handed in. I found the math work especially strange. Addition, subtraction, multiplication and division were also done on lined paper. The various numerical columns were all over the place, veering left and right. In our little school back home, we used graph paper for math problems, and all numbers were entered neatly one below the other – less chance of error and much easier to work with!

Beginning with the fourth grade, we had a notebook for each subject. Whenever a homework assignment had to be handed in, we handed in the complete notebook. Nothing was torn out. In this way, the teacher and the parents always had a complete overview of what the student had done throughout the year. Each assignment was graded and accounted for – no nonsense about how the teacher might have lost the work that the student insisted he had handed in. (Sound familiar, teachers?)

It was in January of the next year that I was asked to go down to the office. I was scared because being called to the office usually meant that the student was in trouble. In those days, the principal still spoke to the student herself. She was the disciplinarian and counselor, all rolled into one. My visit to the office turned out to be quite interesting. I was introduced to a middle-aged couple and their teenage son, Adolf. They had just arrived from Germany and knew even less English than I did. I was asked to interpret the boy's grades. The German report card is done numerically, 1 being an A, 2 a B, etc. His grades were all very good. Now I finally had someone with whom I could converse fluently. Soon thereafter, a boy arrived from Italy. His name was Rainieri. Not much later two more boys arrived, also from Germany. Now we had five foreigners in the school. During recess, the five of us became quite an attraction. We would stand in a large circle and skillfully kick a soccer ball from one to another, make it bounce off our heads, flick it on to the next boy with a snap of the head, all of this without the ball ever touching the ground. The American kids had never seen anything like this before – soccer was then still a totally unfamiliar sport to most Americans. Although all of us were fairly good players, (we all continued at the college level, and I was the captain of the Roosevelt University team) it was the boy named Willy who became a professional soccer player. He played for the Chicago Sting and was selected to the United States Olympic Team and National Team and later became the coach of the United States National Team.

The five of us became well known in the school. Willy and his brother were excellent musicians. They played the accordion beautifully. Adolf was the mathematics brain; he had soon established a reputation as the best mathematics student in the school. I was the best speller and usually got A's on my compositions. Rainieri and I were also good singers.

We were told, one day, that in the afternoon we would have to take a musical aptitude test. This turned out to be a far more important event than I could have possibly imagined at that time. The test consisted basically of us having to distinguish between different musical pitches. We had to determine which one was higher or lower. That was it! We got the results a few weeks later. I had passed and was invited to learn how to play an instrument for the Kelly High School band or orchestra. Those of us who were accepted into the program now had to list from 1 to 3 the choice of instrument we wanted to learn. I listed the trumpet, clarinet or violin. I included the violin because my father had fiddled around a little in his youth and I knew it would please him. When the music teacher came, he said, "I see you want to play the violin. That's wonderful. We always need more violin players. We have plenty of clarinets and trumpets." That was that, and when I got to high school, I learned how to play the violin.

My high school years went by fast. I played in the orchestra and sang in the choir. I joined the ROTC in my third year and made the rank of captain before I graduated.

Somewhere in some old photo album I have several pictures of me in my uniform proudly displaying the medals that I earned. Funny how fast history changes – I have pictures of my father and my uncles in German WWII uniforms, and here I am in an Ike jacket with American medals on my chest. I was an average student who never really tried his best. My grades were okay, but nothing to brag about. I began to work in a Certified grocery store when I turned sixteen and kept this job through my college years. The boss was very kind to me and let me work full time during vacations, part-time during the school year. I could always take off during examination time.

It was in my last year of high school that Miss Corrigan, our English teacher, asked every student in class where he or she was going to go to college. Most students had picked their college and some replied that they were going to become either policemen, firemen or learn some other trade.

When she came to me, I didn't know what to say. I had never seriously considered going to college. To go to such an advanced school, a university, that was for special people, certainly not for an immigrant kid like myself. When Miss Corrigan noticed my hesitation, she very tactfully and gently told me that I should definitely apply to a college. She explained that I had the ability and that I owed it to myself and my parents to give it a try. I did give it a try and I still thank this kind and caring teacher for giving me the confidence that I needed to go and pursue a university education, the first one in my family to do so.

During all of this time, my parents, brother and I attended the church whose pastor had played such an important role in establishing us in Chicago. As more and more immigrant families

arrived, we had an ever-increasing number of young people in our congregation. We, the slightly older ones, thought it would be a good idea to involve these new arrivals from ages fourteen and up to be more active in the church. We started a youth group and invited these young people to participate. On the night of our first meeting, we noticed that there were quite a few that did not attend. After a few phone calls, we learned that their parents were afraid to let their kids travel alone by bus at night. That was understandable. A few of us older young men already had cars. I had inherited my brother's 1958 Chevy. We now decided that those of us with cars would pick up the younger kids, those who were on our "route." My group consisted of three girls: Angie, Karin and Ingrid. Why am I telling you this? This "ride to youth group" led to the best thing that ever happened to me in all my life. How? After these rides had gone on for quite some time, Ingrid, the prettiest and smartest one of the three, asked me if I would like to go with her to the spring musical at her high school. They were producing Oklahoma. She wanted to see this production but her parents would not allow her to go by herself at night on the bus. We went and had a great time. Now I asked her to go with me. I don't remember where, but the rest is history. We were married in 1969 by the same pastor who had done so much for her and my family. Our marriage was blessed with two wonderful children who are now also happily married.

My teaching career was most interesting. I taught one year in grammar school – kindergarten. What an experience this was. The principal liked me and told me that I could always come back and teach there. I was grateful, but I took the job as German teacher at Tilden High School. That school had been one of the premier schools in the city when it was known as Tilden Tech. When I got there, it was in the midst of a racial change. There were fights every day. During one riot, we had 300 blue helmeted riot police surrounding the building. There was a commotion outside my room one day. When I went to see what was going on, I saw two girls facing each other. One had an 8-inch butcher knife in her hand. (The home economics room was next to my room.) I don't know if I would do this today, but on that day, I slowly approached the girl with the knife, gently, but firmly, put my hand on her wrist that held the knife, and said, "You will give me that, won't you?" After what seemed an eternity, she nodded, and I was able to take the knife from her. The crowd dispersed. I knew that some of the bystanders were disappointed in this non-violent end to the incident.

I taught German for a year at the LaSalle Language Academy, the first public school in Chicago where students learned a foreign language beginning in kindergarten. One year later, I was asked to be the program's coordinator for this language program, which would run from kindergarten through Grade 12. When the funding ended two years later, I became the German teacher at Lincoln Park High School where I taught German for the next 20 years. This was an absolute delight. I had some of the brightest students from throughout the city. Almost every year, we took an extended field trip to Germany, Switzerland, Austria, and crossed into France to see Paris, Milan, Venice and Verona in Italy.

While at Lincoln Park, I started a string group, which is now the orchestra. There are presently more than 250 students playing string instruments.

As the founder, I have been asked to compose and conduct a piece of my composition for each concert. I thoroughly enjoy this. Every year a string player receives a scholarship in my name to participate in a summer string program. I also compose and conduct pieces for our church choir. All of this has been made possible because of those music classes at Kelly High School. I thank Mr. Blackard still today for teaching me the rudiments of violin playing. That was the key to my involvement in music, which has given me so much joy and pleasure until this very day.

There is a German saying that asks a question and provides a very wise answer:

Wer ist der glücklichste auf Erden?

Der, der nicht wünscht noch glücklicher zu werden.

(Who is the happiest person in the world?

He, who does not wish to become any happier.)

Using this criteria, in which I believe, by the way, I see myself indeed as the luckiest and happiest man in the world. From very tenuous beginnings, (my mother told me that as a baby I was near death's door several times) through an extremely poor childhood, to having to adjust to a new way of life - all along I have been blessed - blessed with deeply caring parents; the best wife in the world, wonderful children and many good friends. It was due to that humble beginning that I learned to appreciate every good thing that came my way and not to expect anything for nothing.

I thank everyone who touched my life and gave me new reasons to carry on. I thank America for giving this timid, little boy a new chance at a new life, even though I still remember Chuck and some of my new American friends gently knocking on my head and saying, "Hi, Helmet."

The great writer Goethe once stated, "By what a writer says he shows his style; by what he leaves unsaid, he shows his wisdom."

Well, dear friends, this is my story. I think it is a good story, because it is a story of a good life.

But is it interesting? Is it an interesting story? That, my friends, is not for me to say. I leave that for you to judge – but whatever you decide, I know that in your verdict, you will be kind.

THE VIOLIN

It all started with an accident. That accident, two years ago – and yes, I still call it an accident. Two fingers chopped off just above the middle joints. If you don't call that an accident, what would you call it? Of course, the company lawyers used the term "self-inflicted" a lot, and they tried their best to prove it. The blade had to have come down this way, and the hand would have to have been placed like this – very unnatural, etc., etc. They raised their voices and made accusations, while Mr. Sniffle Nose, my boss, just sat there and stared at me all the time, as if he could somehow intimidate me, like he had done so often on the job. I kept my eyes lowered, just as I had been told to do, but I felt his eyes burning on the top of my head. That's okay, asshole, I thought to myself, keep on staring; stare all you want, you're not scaring me. Once in a while, I would put my bandaged hand on the table, just to make it clear that I was the injured party here, the victim, injured physically and mentally. Scarred for life, that's what my lawyer said. I like that. That was powerful – scarred for life.

The whole thing was over in three hours. I was awarded one-half of what my lawyers were asking. One-half, that doesn't sound so good, does it? But my lawyers were bastards, too, just like those pompous asses that represented the company. One-half of the outrageous figures they were asking for was still a lot more than I ever expected to get. How much was one-half? Well, let's just say, up into seven figures.

The first thing I did was quit my job. I'm sure that in one way or another they would have found some reason to fire me. I didn't want to give them that satisfaction, especially Mr. Sniffle Nose, that uptight ass, who had been jerking me around for some time now. I know he never liked me, but the feeling was mutual.

After a few days of just hanging around the house I came to the conclusion that I had to move away from here. I had nothing against the old neighborhood, but somehow everything just seemed crowded and grungy, and a few people had already asked me about the settlement concerning my accident. I told them that the court hadn't yet decided. I know some of these people were going to hit me up for money. I had to get out of here fast.

Chicago is a beautiful city – well, at least some parts of it are beautiful. The lakefront is gorgeous. Michigan Avenue is, as they say, magnificent. There are beautiful tree-lined streets in neighborhoods where meticulously maintained houses cost millions of dollars. The one thing I had always wanted, more than anything else, was a place to live that had a view over the lake;

somewhere along Lake Shore Drive, facing east, to see the rising sun would be ideal.

I soon found a real estate agent that dealt with properties in the Gold Coast area and called to make an appointment. The slightly puzzled look on the receptionist's face was unmistakable when I introduced myself and stated that I had an appointment with Ms. Schuler. I was asked to have a seat. Two minutes later, a very elegant lady came out from one of the offices and introduced herself. If she was disappointed in her prospective client, she didn't let on. It didn't take long for me to find out why she was so gracious toward me – she had done her homework and knew all about my settlement.

After she had asked me to take a seat on the other side of her huge desk, she asked me if I would like some refreshments – I declined. She asked me what I was specifically looking for in this part of town. I told her that the place didn't have to be big, but it had to be high enough so that I could get a good view of the lake, see Lake Shore Drive in both directions, and preferably be right off Oak Street Beach. Any kind of balcony would make it even better.

At first, I was a little disappointed when I was told that out of the three lawyers who were assigned to represent me in my bodily injury lawsuit that it would be Ms. Kinsky, a forty something, short lady, with a rather kind looking face who would be the lead attorney in my case. I had nothing against her personally; she just didn't look aggressive enough to really fight for me tooth and nail. I soon learned, however, that I had misjudged her. She was smart, really smart.

After I had been introduced to the entire team, she led me to her office. I had to tell once again the whole story behind the accident. All of this had been written down before, but she made me tell it again. She hardly looked at me while I was talking and, in my opinion, wrote down a lot more than what was really important. She began to ask me questions about my parents (both deceased) and siblings (none), early childhood experiences and extra-curricular activities in high school. I didn't play any sports, but I sang in the chorus and played the violin in the school orchestra. She held up her hand and looked up.

"Stop, stop right there," she said. "You played the violin in the school orchestra?"

I nodded. Was that so hard to believe? A smile came across her face, a bright smile, and now she actually looked pretty.

"Tell me again what you just said."

"I played the violin in high school." I repeated my statement.

"How many years did you play?"

"One year in beginning orchestra and two in advanced," I replied.

"Advanced? You must have been pretty good."

"Not really. I sat all the way in back of the second violin section." I confessed.

"You played in the advanced orchestra, so you were quite good, do you understand?"

I nodded.

"Did you continue playing after you graduated?"

"Not that much. It wasn't so much fun playing by myself."

"But you played. And you enjoyed playing until this accident, right?" She nodded her head ever so gently while looking right into my eyes.

"Yes," I said. I understood.

"Do you still have your violin?" she asked.

"Yes, in my closet. It is dusty and some of the strings are broken." I answered.

"Tomorrow, you bring the violin to me." Her voice was authoritative. "We'll take care of it. You really miss not being able to play the violin, don't you?" Again she nodded her head slightly, as she continued to look straight at me.

"Yes, I really do miss not being able to play my violin." I firmly responded.

"Good," she said. "You are a single man, no parents, no brothers or sisters, and since the accident, you see your friends even less than before, right?"

"Right!" I affirmed.

"And the only real joy left in your life was your violin, right?"

"Right!" I said with conviction, as I looked right back into her smiling face.

"Good," she said softly. "You love your violin, you love playing it; you love the way the music makes you feel, but now...?" She looked at me with wide-open eyes.

"Yes," I said, "you are absolutely right. That is my greatest loss," and I made a face as if I was about to cry.

"Good," she said, "Just don't overdo it."

Ms. Schuler had three places for me to look at, all condos on Lake Shore Drive. Perfect for any single man. I loved all three of them. But now I was a rich single man and I could afford to be picky. One was a little too far from the beach. One was on the third floor; not high enough for me to get the view I wanted. Condo number three, however, was just perfect – seventeenth floor, balcony, and a block from Oak Street Beach. Surprisingly, it wasn't even the most expensive of the three properties. Method of payment? Cash, of course. Since the apartment was completely furnished, I moved in on the first of the month.

As instructed, I brought my violin with me to court. Ms. Kinsky had it repaired. It was in better condition than ever before. The violin lay on the table in front of Ms. Kinsky. I repeatedly placed my bandaged hand on the table, not too obviously, but openly enough for the jury to get a good look at it. After the details of the accident had been presented again, Ms. Kinsky began to question me:

"Are your parents still living?"

"No."

"Do you have any siblings?"

"No."

"Are you married?"

"No."

"What high school did you attend?"

"Kelly High School."

"Were you a good student?"

"So-so."

"Did you play sports?"

"No."

"What was your favorite subject?"

"Orchestra."

"What instrument did you play?"

"Violin."

"How many years did you play in the orchestra?"

"Three."

"Did you continue to play after you graduated?"

"Yes."

"Do you listen to violin music?"

"Yes, I have all of the great concertos."

"Can you name some?"

"Tchaikovsky, Brahms, Mendelssohn, Beethoven, Mozart's Third, Paganini."

Ms. Kinsky looked around the courtroom. She then turned directly to the jury and said, "Please excuse me for asking my client this question, but it has to be asked."

She paused.

"Do you miss playing your violin?"

I looked down and mumbled, "Yes, very much."

"Let me ask you again, and this time answer a little louder, please. Do you miss playing your violin?"

It was not difficult for me to answer this question in a truly sad voice, because I did miss the high school orchestra, and especially Kate, the girl for whom I actually joined the orchestra; Kate, that pretty and friendly girl, who wound up sitting right in front of me. Kate, who would occasionally talk to me, especially when she needed help with her algebra.

"Yes, I do, very much so."

"No further questions, your honor."

And now came the part that I believe really swung the jury over to me. One of the three-piece suit guys from the insurance company got up and approached the desk where Ms. Kinsky and I were sitting. He pointed to the violin case, looked at me and said, "I, too, am a friend of the violin, and I admire your choice of violin music that you have collected. But tell me, why don't you have the violin concerto by Schubert?"

"Objection," cried Ms. Kinsky, as she jumped from her chair. "Counsel wants to trick my client because he knows perfectly well, as does my client, that Schubert never wrote a violin concerto."

There was a gasp from the audience and some members of the jury shook their heads. The three-piece suit guy was embarrassed. Ms. Kinsky was smart, really smart!

My new life suited me just fine. After I got up in the morning, all I had to worry about was how to spend my day. My financial advisor had assured me that with the way my money was invested, I would never have to worry about it again – the interest alone would go a long way. I would hardly ever need to touch the principal. Since I lived right in the middle of the city, I did not go and buy myself a fancy new car. I didn't need one. I did, however, buy some new clothes. Again, nothing fancy, but I did want to look decent.

My greatest pleasure was to stroll down Michigan Avenue toward the river. Sometimes I would just walk on all the way to Millennium Park or the Art Institute. Most of the time, though, I stayed on the Magnificent Mile.

There is a lovely little park by the Water Tower. That is where I would often sit on one of the benches and watch the people walk by, or I would observe the people who were sitting on the other benches. Sometimes I would find a comfortable spot right by the Wrigley Building and from there, too, watch the people as they came and went. I did not know that there were so many tourists in Chicago – and I don't mean people from other parts of the country. No – people from all over the world. The Japanese were the most conspicuous, usually in groups led by an energetic tour guide, who seemed to be in total control. People in the group followed like obedient sheep. Then there were the Europeans: the French were the loudest; the Germans, the most eager to take everything in; the British always had an air of superiority about them, but I did not see that many of them. The Spanish-speaking people were usually outgoing, very talkative and laughed the loudest. I enjoyed these days tremendously, content just to see the world go by.

And then it happened. Believe me, I will never forget this moment. I had been sitting on a bench in Water Tower Park, just watching the people around me, as I usually do, when a very well dressed elderly gentleman sat down on the opposite bench. His dark gray suit was obviously tailor made, his shirt and tie, exquisite. His shoes were of the finest soft Italian leather, and on his head he wore a hat of checkered material, with a silver emblem on the left side, from which protruded a dainty red feather. He was so elegant that no matter how hard I tried not to be obvious, my eyes were simply drawn to him. My, my, I thought, aren't you a picture of elegance? How much did that outfit set you back? As I sat there trying not to look at him, I "HEARD" a voice say – 'look all you want. At least I know how to dress. You annoy me.' At that moment, the man got up and walked away.

I sat there stunned. What had just happened? Did I imagine that voice, those words? Did I just think that this is what the man could have said about me? But that voice – I heard a real voice, as real as if the man had actually spoken to me, and yet I knew that he had not uttered a single word. I sat there for a while trying to get this experience out of my head. Just a weird experience, that's all, I told myself. Just forget about it.

About a week later, it happened again. It was a beautiful, warm day in Chicago and I had walked down to Oak Street Beach where I took a seat in the outdoor café that is now put up there every summer. I ordered an ice tea and did my usual thing – that is, people watching. Children played in the sand, others waded waist deep in the water; in the distance, a few well-tanned young people played beach volleyball – a perfect day to be at the beach. As I let my eyes wander over this magnificent scene, I saw a woman in a bikini come walking toward the café. She caught my eye immediately. She was absolutely stunning with a tremendous figure wearing a very daring bikini for a Chicago beach. I watched her as she approached the café and then make a sharp left turn so that she walked right past me. Very nice, I thought to myself. Yes, baby, you got it all. Go ahead, strut your stuff. When she had walked a few steps past me, I "HEARD" a female voice say – 'Jerk! Put your eyes back in your head, you loser!'

My jaw dropped! That was her speaking to me, but she hadn't said a single word. That was not just a voice in my head. I had really heard a female voice say those words – as real as if she had said them right to my face. I looked after her, but by now she had disappeared among the people crowding the refreshment stand.

I sat there for a long time with all kinds of thoughts racing through my head. Was I hearing things that weren't being said out loud? Was I imagining that these two people were saying things that I expected them to say? Was I beginning to crack? Maybe I should have stayed at my job or found some other kind of work so that my mind would be more occupied. Was I spending too much time alone? I dismissed all of these thoughts because those two voices had been so real, so human, that they could not have simply been imagined by me!

It happened again, only four days later. I was sitting in the café in Millennium Park. At the next table sat a very attractive woman with her two daughters. I took her to be in her mid-thirties and the girls at about thirteen and ten. All were very pretty and enjoying each other's company. They were eating ice cream. My eyes strayed over to the charming group repeatedly and I thought to myself, what a happy, lovely family. It must be nice to be her husband and father to those pretty two girls. As I took another sip of my latté, I "HEARD" a voice say – 'what a pervert! Looks just like a pervert! He's got nothing else to do but stare at us? We'll leave as soon as possible.' I looked up and saw her looking at me, while the older girl was saying something to both of them. The mother had not spoken a word, and yet I had clearly "HEARD" her voice! I was not imagining! She had SPOKEN to me! I waved the waiter over, paid my bill and left. I had to get away from there. This was beginning to scare me, really scare me!

I walked the streets of Chicago for the next three days as if I were in a daze. I did not dare look at anyone directly or let my mind form a thought about any person I saw. While I was eating in a restaurant, I kept my eyes down on my food, or if I looked up, I hummed a melody in my head, or looked at the pictures on the walls. I did everything I could not to think about any of the people I saw.

My confidence had returned again and I was ready to try an experiment. I would single out a few people and concentrate on them. If I got no response, fine; but if I "HEARD" that person speak back to me, then I would know that I was not just imaging this – then, there would be a real problem.

The next day, one of those sparkling Indian summer days in Chicago, I walked along Michigan Avenue, all the way down to the Art Institute. I went inside and leisurely strolled from one gallery to the next. The Impressionists, as usual, got most of my attention. I could never stop to marvel at the world-class collection that was presented here in the prairie land of America's Midwest. After filling my eyes and mind with the beautiful scenes, I went to the courtyard café, one of my favorite places for people watching. After my latté and chocolate croissant, I looked around for a suitable subject. I rejected the elderly gentleman with the newspaper – he was too occupied with himself. The mother with her little boy was also rejected. The boy was just too much of a handful for her to think of anything else. I spied three young people a few tables down from me. A man and two women were holding a lively conversation. They looked as if they could be students at the School of the Art Institute. If they weren't, they really tried very hard to look as if they were. I couldn't hear what they were saying, but whatever they were discussing, they were really into it.

I watched them more intently now, trying to figure out from their gestures and facial expressions what their subject matter might be. I deliberately concentrated on them, just to prove to myself that my previous experiences had been some sort of fluke, some trick that my mind was playing on me. I looked most intently at the brunette; the one, who sat directly facing me. What made her stand out from the other two was her hat – it was a special forces green beret, with a blue emblem in front. This beret was at such a steep angle over her right ear that it was surprising it did not slide off her head. She obviously had it pinned down in some way. Along with the hat, she wore a ruffled white blouse, which hung loosely over a pair of frayed jeans. Her bare feet were clad in green clogs. The whole outfit was obviously designed to shock any fashionista and to accentuate her individuality and bohemian, 'I don't give a damn what you think' attitude. Her reddish-brown hair hung straight down along the side of her face. She sat very straight and still, but her eyes moved quickly back and forth between her two companions. She listened more than she spoke. Despite the fact that she looked a little strange at first glance, there was something charming about her. She seemed like a person who would be fun to know.

I kept my eyes fixed on her while all these thoughts ran through my head. I looked at her and tried not to think of anything. That, of course, was not possible. New thoughts entered my mind – how old was she? What was her relationship to the other two? She sure had a pretty smile. She was probably quite intelligent. As I looked down to pick up my latté, I suddenly heard a voice, a very pleasant voice. I looked up and saw her looking at me. And then, distinctly, I "HEARD" the voice say – 'I wish he would stop looking at me! He gives me the creeps! Doesn't he have anything better to do than to stare at me? Probably thinks I'm crazy or just weird. Probably couldn't imagine that I have talent, real talent. Guys like that annoy the hell out of me!' All this time she had been looking at me and, of course, she had not spoken a single word. The young man next to her touched her arm and all three got up and left the café. No backward glance from her.

My mind was numb. I gathered my thoughts slowly. This could just not be true. There was a pattern here. For some unexplainable reason, people could sense that I was thinking about them. They obviously did not know what I was thinking about, otherwise their thoughts would not be so negative. Hadn't I only thought positively about them? Well, maybe the chick in the bikini – but even about her, my thoughts had been nothing but flattering.

What could I do? What should I do? I know, most people would tell me to go see a doctor, maybe even a shrink. That was out of the question. I was not sick. I was not deranged. There was just something happening that I did not understand. Why was this happening now? It never happened before. Did it have something to do with the accident? Did I maybe have a guilty conscience? I don't think so. Why should I? Just look at my left hand. Me? Guilty? I think not!

By now it was late fall and signs of the brutal Chicago winter were all too apparent. The flower boxes along Michigan Avenue were empty, the trees had shed their leaves. Occasionally, I would walk along the lakeshore, but after a cold spray of water pounding the walking path soaked me, I gave that up, too. If I was to leave my apartment at all, it would have to be to somewhere indoors, but somehow I dreaded being among other people. This disturbed me because it was precisely that, the watching, the observing, letting the mind wonder about the people I saw; it was exactly this that I had enjoyed most in my leisure hours. There was no way around it. I had to go out again and take my chances. I would try to think about everything else except the people who were there in the same room with me.

My first new venture out was to the Bloomingdale's lobby. Here there was a coffee bar with just a few tables set behind it. The advantage of this place was that although it was very busy, most people just picked up their coffees with some pastry and then moved on. Once in a while, someone would sit down at one of the tables. They would not stay long, however, a sip or two of coffee, a quick glance at the paper and they were off. This was a good spot for me to test at least one observation about what had happened to me with these voices that I heard. In each case, I had specifically concentrated on that person a little longer than just a normal quick passing thought. I had quite deliberately zeroed in on that person and in my mind formulated a series of thoughts about him or her. What would happen if I shifted my attention away from a person as soon as one or two thoughts about that person had formed in my mind? Would it be possible for anyone to "SPEAK" to me without me having made the first concentrated contact? The coffee bar seemed to be the ideal spot for this experiment.

I ordered a latté and a cranberry scone, took a newspaper from the rack, and sat down at a table from which I could see most people as they came and went. Some stopped briefly, took a careful sip of their hot beverage, and then hurried on their way. I would look at my paper once in a while, read a paragraph or two and then look at the people seated at the other few tables. I would close my eyes and listen to the music piped in from somewhere. All the time, I took care not to dwell on one individual or one thought too long. I did this for more than an hour and was relieved to learn that I did not "HEAR" anyone "TALK" to me. It was now clear that I would only "HEAR" from the other person if that person somehow sensed that I was in some way occupied with him or her.

Although I did not feel good about it, I knew that I had to do the experiment one more time. If the other person would "TALK" to me, then I knew for sure that something was terribly wrong. To do this, I chose the always-crowded food court at Water Tower Place. I got myself two tacos and a coke, sat down at an empty table close to the middle of the establishment and looked around the room for a suitable subject. It had to be a person who was not too occupied with other people, reading material, or anything else.

I immediately eliminated adults with kids and groups of teenagers. They were just too busy with themselves. My eyes stopped on a woman sitting alone sipping a cup of coffee. She was doing the same thing I was doing – looking around the room without having anything in particular to do. I was close enough to see her quite well and yet far enough away so that my observation of her was not too obvious.

She appeared to be in her mid-forties, dressed very elegantly with perfectly styled hair. Her large gold earrings were matched to the gold ring on her right hand. Her tailored cornflower-blue dress was a little daring in its shortness, and afforded a good view of her shapely legs. Her imported Italian calfskin shoes looked expensive. I liked everything I saw.

I let my eyes wander about the room, but every few seconds I would come back to her and form a thought about her; she is quite elegant – her outfit is very stylish – what a beautiful woman, she must have been a very lovely girl – is she married to a rich man? (no wedding band) – is she highly successful? – self-confident – probably very pleasant – I wish she would smile – I bet she has a pretty smile. I would occasionally look away, but then zero in on her again and form another thought – I wonder if she is waiting for someone – she doesn't seem to be in a hurry – I like the way she sips her coffee.

Now she was looking straight at me and I "HEARD" her voice say – 'You are obviously a very bored man. If you think you looking at me flatters me, you're mistaken. You disturb me. I didn't come here to be gawked at. If Roberta doesn't show up soon, I'll just have to leave and wait outside for her. I can't take that lunatic much longer.'

The voice stopped when she turned her eyes away from me. I put my head between my hands and sat there dumbfounded. This definitely proved it. People could somehow sense that I was thinking about them. In return, their thoughts about me were negative every time – no matter how positive my thoughts were about them. I felt tears well up in my eyes. I covered them, oblivious to everything around me.

It took me several days to get over this frightening experience. How was it possible that people could tell I was thinking about them? And how was it possible I could "hear" their thoughts? Why did everyone misjudge me so? No one so far had a positive or pleasant thought about me. Did I really come across as such an awful person? Was I that hard to look at? Did I exude an air of unpleasantness? If that was the case, I couldn't understand why. I was dressed stylishly. I showered twice a day. I was clean-shaven and my hair was properly trimmed. Why couldn't anyone have a positive thought about me?

I decided to go back to the old neighborhood and see how my former buddies were doing.

Maybe I could get a clue as to what was going on. Perhaps one of them would "TELL" me something good about me. I came to the conclusion that it would probably be best if I saw them one at a time – that way there would be no confusion of thoughts and I could concentrate strictly on one person. I decided that Sid would be the best choice to start with. I had always considered him to be my best friend. If I got any feedback from him, and if that should be positive, then I would consider meeting some of the others. There were only two other people I could think of, Bob and Peter.

I called Sid and we agreed to meet the following Tuesday night at the Dew Drop Inn. When I arrived at seven, he was already sitting in one of the old booths nursing a beer. He didn't get up to greet me. I sat down and also ordered a beer. I hadn't seen him now for more than two years, but somehow he looked different than I remembered him. His skin was ashen gray and he must have lost some hair. His eyes seemed to have sunken deeper into their sockets. His teeth did not look too good, either. I asked him how he was doing. He told me that everything was fine, but that he moved back home to be with his mother who had the early stages of Alzheimer's. He spent most of his time, when he wasn't working, taking care of her as best he could. I knew he had been married once and was now divorced. His dad had died long ago. He told me that he still worked as the assistant manager down at the supermarket, but lately they had cut back his hours so that he worked at almost a part-time basis. He didn't complain, but I could easily imagine that financially he wasn't doing well, especially with the high cost of medication that his mother needed.

I asked him if he wanted to order a pizza, but he said that he'd just have another beer. I ordered two more beers. As we talked about this and that, I couldn't help but think that for some reason I had always felt sorry for him. He just never seemed really happy, joking around like some of the other guys. There had always been this air of melancholy about him. I could never explain why that would be so. Was I the only person who felt that way about him?

We talked for a little more than an hour and I noticed that during all this time, he did not ask me a single question about myself. I did not volunteer any information because that might seem as if I was boasting, and I definitely did not want to talk to him about my "problem." I told him that it was good to see him again; I wished him the best, we shook hands and I put a twenty-dollar bill on the table. As I began to walk away, I resolved to send him some money in the future.

Just before I reached the door, I "HEARD" his voice from behind me say, 'Same cheap old bastard. I never really did like him. Always thought he was smarter than me. Well, hell with him. Just go! Get out of here!'

For just a moment, I stood there, frozen – but then I pushed open the heavy door and stepped out into the bitter cold night. Only much later, just before I reached home, did I notice that a gentle snow had begun to fall.

Needless to say, I did not call my other buddies. I did not send Sid any money, either. So this is how he saw me? True, I had never really been close to any of them, but I thought they were my friends. He called me cheap. Well, back then I didn't have much more money than any one of the guys. We were all struggling. I had the good fortune that my parents were able to help me make it through school, but everything else I did on my own. I worked for every penny I made. Now I was rich and quite honestly, I earned that, too!

The winter had been long and dreary. I had hardly left my apartment. I would spend hours looking out over the lake and even though the scene never changed, I did not get tired of the view. Quite honestly, I never really took in the scene that was offered me. I mostly sat in front of the big picture window, in a semi-stupor, not really aware of anything. I would only notice that once again it had gotten dark outside and also dark inside. I would then go to my bedroom, lie down fully dressed on my bed and wait for sleep to come.

It took a long time for spring to arrive, but gradually the water in the lake began to look green again. I occasionally saw one of those long Great Lakes steamers on the horizon, slowly chugging along, bringing their cargo to Gary or returning from there to Milwaukee or to Escanaba or points beyond. Now I went out once in a while, and if the sun was warm enough, I would sit on a bench in Water Tower Park. Sometimes I would go as far as Millennium Park and drink a latté in the Park Café. I avoided looking at people and even thinking about any of them. I shut myself off to the outside world. I had always been somewhat of a loner, but now I was completely isolated. I didn't want to think about them, and I did not want to know what they thought about me. I didn't need them! This quiet life, without concern, opinion or judgment about anyone else, was just fine with me. As far as I was concerned, they could all go to hell! I was set for life. I didn't need anyone!

It was on a beautiful warm Saturday afternoon when I decided that it would be a good idea to go to the Art Institute. A leisurely stroll through the galleries filled with masterpieces of the great artists would be good for me. Afterwards, a light meal in the garden café, with perhaps a glass of refreshing wine – maybe a Riesling – would be the perfect way to spend the rest of this lovely day.

I wandered through the galleries for two hours and then made my way to the café where I was pleasantly surprised to see that my favorite table was unoccupied. I asked the perky young waitress if it was all right for me to sit there, which was answered with a cheery, "but, of course." I had just put down the menu – my choice had fallen on the Quiche Lorraine with a glass of Riesling – when I looked up and nearly froze. There, in the farthest corner of the place, sat Mr. Sniffle Nose and his wife. I knew it was his wife, because I had met her once before at an office Christmas party. She seemed like a nice lady. I had wondered what had attracted her to that grouch; the man I called Mr. Sniffle Nose, because he was always dabbing at his nose. It seemed he and his wife were also still waiting for their food, because their table was empty, except for the two water glasses in front of them. I had every urge to get up and walk out, but I had just ordered, and it wouldn't be right to leave now. If I did, I certainly could not show my face around here again. I did not want to risk that. Within a minute or so, their food arrived and they began to eat. I tried not to look at them or think about them, but my thoughts kept returning to Mr. Sniffle Nose. I really never understood why I didn't like him. Quite honestly, he didn't treat me badly. There was just this unexplainable something about him that rubbed me the wrong way, and I don't mean the sniffling nose, either. Why, I had quite often asked myself, did he get a promotion and not me? I had been with the company longer than he had. I understood the business better than he did. I did my job well – I was never late, never missed a day and stayed late when asked. But I wasn't an ass-kisser! Yes, that's right, Mr. Sniffle Nose, I wasn't an ass-kisser like some other people I know. And I wasn't such a snazzy dresser. I didn't always bring a birthday gift for our secretaries. So, all right, Mr. Sniffle Nose, I grant you that. You were more of a people person than I was. So what! That's you and this is me. I hope you're happy!

I had gotten pretty worked up even though that was the last thing I wanted to do. I just couldn't help myself – the way he sat there, all smug with his nice wife, and yes, he still dabbed his nose every so often.

My food arrived and I began to eat. Although I knew that my meal was as good as it always was, I didn't taste any of it. I kept my face down and mechanically took bite after bite washing it down with an occasional gulp of wine. All I wanted to do was to get out of there.

I only had two or three more mouthfuls left on my plate, when I "HEARD" his voice – 'Oh, my God, it's him; it's really him. All that money and he still doesn't look very happy – and as always – he's alone. Funny thing is, I never disliked him at all. But for some reason, I can't help feeling that he had hated me right from the beginning. He didn't even notice that several times I gave him the better assignment or arranged it so that he could have the holidays off when other people had to work. I wonder what would have happened if he had known that Mr. Jayson had told me that he was considering him for a promotion as soon as Mr. Cruz retired. I had agreed with him that that was an excellent idea; that he was a good man who always gave his best for the company. But then he had his accident. Can't play the violin anymore, really? Well, my friend, you got your money – be happy.'

When I looked up for a few seconds, I saw that his wife had raised her wine glass, which she gently clinked with his. She leaned toward him and he gave her a gentle kiss. They seemed to be totally oblivious to their surroundings. I asked for my bill, gave a generous tip and left quickly through the side entrance.

I don't go out much at all anymore. I spend most of my time in front of the window, or, if it is really nice, outside. I sit on my balcony and look at the changing colors of Lake Michigan. I watch the Great Lakes steamers in the distance as they move slowly from left to right or from right to left. Occasionally, I do walk down Michigan Avenue, but I keep my eyes lowered – I don't want to see the faces of the people as they come towards me. When I do eat out, I usually go to busy, noisy places where I can look around the room, but not wind up concentrating on anyone in particular. I have become totally indifferent to the world around me. I don't wonder any longer why this person looks so sad or what makes that person so cheerful. I don't care! It makes no difference to me! You go your way and I'll go my way, all right?

And on one windy autumn morning, I took my violin case and walked to Diversey Harbor. Right where the waves hit against the concrete breakwaters, I threw the case, with the violin in it, as far as I could into the churning waters of the big, cold lake. I stood there in the blustering wind for some time. I watched the case slowly drift further and further out into the icy waters. When I was not able to see it anymore, I turned and walked home.

The days and nights come and go in the same monotonous rhythm. I don't count them anymore. It's all the same to me. I let myself be carried along – there are no ups and no downs. I drift along like a capsized boat on a calm sea after a violent storm. I am drifting away and I don't know – don't care – where I'll land.

Sometimes, when I close my eyes, I see my violin case being carried out on choppy waves into that gray, cold lake. But more often, I see that fragile case, with its innocent cargo, like a tiny coffin, deep at the bottom of the lake, where it is always dark and cold; where there is nothing but complete and absolute silence.

IT'S NOT GOING
TO HAPPEN...

Something happened to me a little while ago that has turned my whole world topsy-turvy. I don't like it one bit and, of course, I have to blame someone for it. Actually, I have two people to blame for it – Beethoven and my wife. You might think this to be very strange, especially since one of those two died more than one hundred fifty years ago. And yet, I blame him, too. Let me explain:

We have now lived in this house for thirty-seven years, and obviously some things are in need of remodeling. The kitchen was done two years ago. Part of a wall was knocked down so that there was an open view of the dining room. This made the whole space seem so much larger. The soffit was torn out and new, taller cabinets were installed. A new oak floor was laid down and granite counter tops replaced the old ones. The ceiling was studded with bright can lighting and task lighting was added under the cabinets. All of this was topped off with shiny new state-of-the-art stainless steel appliances.

This year, it was time to attack the family room. The old, dark paneling, that was so popular thirty/forty years ago, had to go. The carpeted floor, with only concrete beneath it, was replaced with a wide-planked natural bamboo floor. Nine can lights were installed in the ceiling with two separate dimmer switches. New insulation was added to the outside wall, as well as to the crawl space floor and walls. One wall was painted in a forest-green color, while the remaining walls were finished in the now very popular gold color. All of the old furniture was given away and was replaced with a black leather recliner sofa, two occasional chairs, which face the sofa, and a glass and chrome rectangular coffee table between them. A new office area, complete with a new computer, desk, wall unit and filing cabinet, replaced the location of the old piano. The long inside wall, where the old television stood, now has a whole wall lined with bookshelves, which holds a sizeable collection of books, as well as memorabilia. Where the Hummel figurine collection wall unit once stood, there is now a cabinet, which holds a 60-inch plasma TV, all done with the needed surround sound installation, thanks to our son, who knows about these things. Two pictures, a watercolor from our cruise to Mexico, and an original poster from our Hamburg/Berlin trip, grace the walls. The new room is just perfect – everything exactly as my wife and I planned it.

So, what does this have to do with my world being turned upside down? That didn't happen when we had the kitchen remodeled. It took me quite a while to figure it out, but I think I have the answer. At least, I hope so, otherwise, something really strange is happening around here!

You see, I am an amateur composer – a very amateur composer. I write simple pieces for orchestra and they are performed at the high school where I used to teach. Occasionally, I also compose songs for our church choir. In my compositions I do not even try for originality – if they come off as sounding "correct" and have a pleasing melody, then that is good enough for me. Since I have been told that my music sounds "nice," I have been encouraged to keep at it. Quite honestly, one of the greatest pleasures in my life, since my retirement, is to put a sheet of music paper on my piano, make myself a cup of latté, and then work at a musical composition. While doing this, I lose all track of time and often my wife has to tear me away from the piano, since my food is getting cold.

Well, that is how it has been until recently, but then something changed. To be sure, when the family room was finished, and all the new furniture had finally arrived, I went back eagerly to the piano, its home now under the big picture window, to start a new piece for orchestra. I had the basic outline all worked out – a slow introduction in the style of Haydn, then suddenly, but after a slight hesitation, a stunning burst into an allegro section, maybe even allegro vivacé. The opening would be strings only, but then a forte entry, complete with winds, trumpets and tympani: this was going to be fun!

My latté stood steaming on the side of the piano. The paper had been properly marked for the instruments that would be used in this piece; key signature: G major, two four time, pianissimo; andante opening, cellos and basses playing a delicate pizzicato.

I sat and stared at the paper. Finally, I took the pencil and started the theme for the first violins. I stopped at eight measures and added the second violin part; the violas would enter a little later; pizzicato only for the cellos. I continued with the next eight measures, this time with violas. Only the bass had not entered yet – that would have to wait until the tutti and would add extra power and weight at the point when all the other instruments joined in at the allegro section.

But it never came to that. Something was wrong with the way I had started the piece. No matter how many variations I tried, I did not wind up at the sudden switch-over point the way I wanted to. I tried one more time, this time in the key of C. The result was the same; when I came to the point where everyone was supposed to enter, something didn't seem right. The whole thing just fell apart. I got up, took my latté from the piano and walked to the sofa in the living room. I sipped at my coffee drink – it was cold. I walked to the kitchen and dumped the usually so tasty brew into the sink. I could have heated it up, but I knew that somehow it just wouldn't taste right.

The next morning, after a leisurely breakfast, I went back to the piano to try my luck again. I went over the parts that I had written up to this point and could find nothing that needed to be changed. Any other version of what I had written would make it worse, at least, as written by me. This was really getting frustrating. Normally, everything flowed quite naturally, especially if I had already carefully worked it out in my mind, as I had also done this time. To be sure, once in a while I was stuck with the orchestration; that was only natural, after all, I am not a trained musician, but usually I would find some sort of solution that I could live with.

I went over the music line by line and then came to that critical point where, after the slow introduction, everything was to be bright, lively and absolutely stunning – but nothing happened. It just wasn't there! I slammed both hands down on the keyboard – the dissonance was painful. I looked up and looked right into the eyes of – Beethoven.

Yes, Beethoven! No, not an imaginary Beethoven, some figment of my imagination – no, the Beethoven we had brought back from Vienna when we visited friends many years ago. Beethoven, head and shoulders in marble, eight inches tall, complete with tousled hair, stern face and penetrating eyes. I looked down at the keyboard and then back at him. Same stern look, but perhaps even a slight sneer on those white, cold lips. I looked at him, he looked at me, and, of course, I was first to look away. Was this the reason I couldn't get my musical thoughts properly organized? It had never happened before. Then it hit me – the bust of Beethoven had not stood on the piano before the remodeling. It had stood high on a bookshelf up in my study, among great and not so great books. I had forgotten that I even had it, but my wife did not. She brought it down and placed it smack in the middle of my upright piano with a gorgeous orchid on either side. She told me about it when she did it, and I agreed that the top of the piano looked beautiful.

Now, I am not a superstitious person, but I could find no other reason for my sudden lack of inspiration. A good psychiatrist could probably give me all sorts of explanations, tell me about everyone having those creative dry spells, even find explanations of why I feel threatened by Beethoven, my insecurities and lack of faith in my own abilities. And he would probably tell me to move the Beethoven bust back to its old place and then see what happens. Well, that's what I did – without telling my wife about it. I just wanted to give it a shot. And you know what happened? Nothing happened, in the truest sense of the word. I stared at the music paper, added a few notes, carefully replayed the piece measure by measure – and then took the paper, crumbled it up and threw it in the wastepaper basket.

Two days later, I went back to the piano, new paper prepared just for strings. Five lines only – first and second violins, viola, cello and double bass. This was going to be something light – my model was Mozart's Eine Kleine Nachtmusik. The opening was all worked out in my mind – and then it happened again. After I put the first measures down on paper, my mind went blank. I thought I had it all worked out, but I just couldn't go on. No matter how I tried, I realized I was stuck, just like I was with the last piece. This was getting serious!

I don't want to become tedious about this whole thing. Let me just say that I tried again and again, and the same thing happened each time. Nothing. Well, I could go to a psychiatrist and see if he could help to get this thing worked out or – and I think this would probably be the better solution. We could return the room to its original state – put the old paneling back on the wall, place the piano back into the corner where our beautiful new office is now located. The ceiling would have to be redone with its one light, and the old ceiling fan would have to be put back. The new bamboo floor would have to be covered by a drab carpet and the walls would have to be repainted to that faded non-descript color, and…, and…, and… .

I look around the room, and I see my wife's beaming face, and I know that none of that is going to happen; nope, that is just not going to happen!

THE LITTLE ANGEL

My very creative and artistic wife makes beautiful jewelry and ornaments, which she calls "baubles." A bauble is something you don't need but would like to have anyway. These baubles are three-inch Styrofoam balls, which she covers with counted-cross stitch and star quilting. The cross-stitch depicts logos and colors of the most popular universities, colleges, high schools, professional sports teams and countries. The country ornaments have a flag on one side with the country's name, and on the other side, she stitches the word or phrase for "hello" in that country's language; for example, "labas" for Lithuania, "dzien dobry" for Poland, or "bonjour" for France. In addition, she also customizes ornaments for weddings, anniversaries, baby's arrival, confirmation, etc.

Besides the ornaments, she also makes beautiful and unique jewelry. She makes the necklaces, bracelets, pendants and earrings from all kinds of gems, stones and crystals, but lately she has begun to make everything almost exclusively using Swarovski crystals from Wattens, Austria. People just love the sparkle and the colors that these crystals produce.

When she first started to make these items, she would occasionally sell them at craft shows at the nearby high schools and church bazaars. Her products proved to be so popular that we decided to sell her creations on a regular basis at the farmer's market in one of the neighboring suburbs from our house. This market runs from mid-May to mid-October – every Saturday from 7 a.m. to 12:30 pm. We have been doing this ever since she retired seven years ago.

We pack up the car on Friday nights. Surprisingly, the tent, two folding tables, two chairs, all the merchandise, etc., fit into our old Honda when we pack everything in a precise and orderly manner. We arrive at the market at around six on Saturday mornings and by seven we have everything set up. My job consists basically of helping with the heavy stuff- the tent and the folding tables. I am also responsible for hanging all the baubles on the right stand according to colleges, universities, professional teams and nationalities, as well as hanging up our company's name banner. The market likes all the vendors to have an identification banner. After I'm finished with my chores, I go and get the coffee.

In the past, I usually took a book along to pass the time while my wife sold her wares. I don't do that anymore. Why? Because there is something much better to do – "people watching." That is the primary reason why I enjoy these Saturday mornings so much, even though the setting is always the same, and although, for the most part, the people are the same, too, there is always something new to discover – and the profits from the sales are nothing to be sneezed at either. We have already taken some very nice cruises and vacations from the money that these Saturday mornings have brought in. If I didn't say it before, let me say it now very emphatically, my wife's artistic creations are very popular and she has a great number of repeat customers. She also gets so many orders that during the summer months she can hardly keep up with production.

But I am there for the people. First of all, there are the other vendors. When we arrive at six, the farmers, who occupy three or four vendor spaces with their fruits and vegetables, are ready to sell. They start their set up at 2 am. Their produce depends on the season, but throughout the spring, summer and fall, you will be able to find the freshest and most delicious peaches, peas, cherries, plums, strawberries, raspberries, blueberries and any other kind of berry you can think of. Here you will find several different varieties of potatoes, fresh corn, cucumbers, zucchini, squash, beans and beets. And in the fall the abundance of pumpkins and apples is everywhere. I love to walk past their displays and smell the dill, always a reminder of my mother making pickles when I was a kid.

There are always two flower vendors, one at each end of the market. One vendor has beautiful pre-arranged bouquets of flowers from roses to daisies and the other vendor has loose-stemmed flowers. You can pick and choose whatever you wish for a special bouquet.

One vendor sells different flavored olive oils and balsamic vinegars. Another one features mild to spicy giardiniera. One man sells homemade pesto and always offers samples. The cheese people will give samples when asked. There are freshly baked cookies and kettle corn available, and a French nun sells the most delicious pastries made in the convent by the sisters to help pay the bills. There is something for everyone at this market; everything ranging from snow cones to pizza and scrumptious paella, brats, spiral shaped French fries and handmade pasta, just to mention a few.

There is a vendor who is known as the knife and scissor sharpener guy, and he is kept quite busy. There are artists who paint, draw and do ceramic creations. And then there are the jewelry vendors. One features Southwestern-style jewelry, while the other is more into the heavy silver and big stone look. We sell jewelry, too, but my wife's creations are more delicate and symmetrical. Her Swarovski crystal bracelets, with their magnetic clasps, are a big hit. They range from extra-small to extra-large and are available in all the birthstone months as well as a rainbow of different colors. The same is true for the pendants and earrings to match.

But her "baubles" are something really special – no one else has a product like this. After seeing a similar product many years ago, she took the idea to another level of artistic design and made this concept all her own. It is truly unique and people are always amazed when they see her colorful creations for the first time. It is interesting to watch people's reactions when they discover their alma mater ornament hanging among all the others, which usually leads to a sale.

There is also live music every Saturday; music ranging from blue grass to jazz and modern show tunes. The performers are all very good and always draw a nice crowd to hear them play. As you can imagine, the Saturday morning market is a lively and fun place to be.

The shoppers can be divided into three different time groups. First, there are the ones that show up right a 7:00 am when the market opens. They know exactly what they want. They go from booth to booth, buy potatoes here, a loaf of bread there, a bunch of flowers at one of the flower vendors and maybe a bar of soap from the soap lady. She makes colorful bars of soap in the most fragrant smells. These shoppers come, and in a few minutes they are gone.

The main bulk of the shoppers come between 9:00 and 11:00 am. These people stroll leisurely along the two long rows of booths (there are usually between 60 to 70 vendors here on any given Saturday), buy something to eat and look at anything and everything that interests them. This group consists mainly of families, whereas the early morning group is made up mostly of housewives getting their shopping out of the way as quickly as possible. This second group also includes many children, and it is interesting to see how these kids know how to manipulate the adults with them. It is always fun to observe grandfathers who are strolling through the market with their granddaughters. They stop at our booth often, because these young girls are immediately attracted to all shiny objects. They stand before the sparkling jewelry and ask politely whether they may pick up a bracelet or try on a pendant. They look up at grandpa and their eyes say "please," and grandpa reaches for his wallet. Our prices are very reasonable and grandfather simply cannot deny them this simple pleasure. In their eyes, he has just become a hero.

The third group of shoppers are the ones that show up around 11:00 am. They seem to be either looking for something to eat, or they are killing time before they go to lunch at one of the several restaurants that are nearby, or are waiting to catch a train to go downtown for an afternoon or evening appointment. They do not come with anything specific in mind, and it is quite infrequent that they buy anything, although it has happened that one or the other was simply fascinated by one of our baubles. They show ecstatic joy in discovering an ornament with the flag of Croatia on it. They love to tell us that grandma came from there many years ago and how she would just love to have this reminder hanging on her Christmas tree. The joy is even more profound when they read the "dobar dan" stitched on the reverse side of the ornament.

The people keep coming all morning long and they are fascinating to watch. Many of them are "repeaters" and we know them either by name or we recognize them from afar. One of them is "Santa Claus" (not his real name), because of his red face and long white beard. He is a pleasant man who always stops at our booth to say hi. Sometimes he purchases an ornament from the rack or orders one of the custom-made colleges or university ornaments for one of his many nephews and nieces or friends' children. He particularly likes the fact that they can be stitched to include their names and graduation year. After he makes his purchases, he frequently comes back with some treat for us from the French nun, to further show his appreciation for our work.

Then there is Bob. That's what I call him. He is a jovial man, who walks briskly through the crowds, stopping here or there to chat with some of the vendors. I always look for him because he usually wears a T-shirt with something written on it. The messages are always funny. My favorite one is "in bed by seven, home by nine."

Another most interesting character is the "Brazilian Millionaire." I don't know if he is a Brazilian or if he is a millionaire. He certainly looks as if he should be both. He is about sixty, tall, a little pudgy, but not fat, with a deep, dark tan. His hair is snow white and a little long at the nape. He sports a neatly trimmed white mustache. He always wears brightly colored pants and a white, open shirt. On his bare feet, he wears very comfortable and expensive looking loafers. His wife usually is with him. She looks like she is in her late thirties. She is pure elegance personified – perfect hair and make up, elegant dress, quite short to reveal her shapely and youthful legs. Her top is always rather open, revealing her equally shapely and youthful "girls." There are two young girls with them of perhaps twelve and nine, who show every indication that they will soon become lovely young ladies, too. I love watching them as the girls flitter from booth to booth, urging their mother to come quickly to see what they have discovered. As the three ladies investigate what they have just found, the "Brazilian Millionaire" strolls on leisurely, looks back at his three "girls," waits patiently, and when summoned, walks back to them, reaching into his back pocket to pull out his wallet.

There is a couple that I enjoy watching every time they come to the market. She, a tall and let me say "robust" woman, walks ahead of her husband, stops at a booth and makes a purchase. She then hands the bag to her husband, who always walks a few steps behind her, stops a few steps behind her, and steps forward when she summons him. He is a short, bald man, who does not seem to know where he is or why he is here. He silently takes what she gives him, and they move on, he always a few steps behind her.

Then there are always the "out of season dressers." I call them that because no matter how cold it may be in the spring or early fall, they show up in short pants, T-shirts and sandals. While we are warmly dressed and still feel the chilly wind, they seem to be absolutely comfortable in their scant attire. And then there is the opposite – no matter how warm or even hot it may be, there are always some people so bundled up as if it were the middle of winter.

And speaking of clothing, oh my word, you would not believe what we get to see. My wife always says, "Don't these people ever look at themselves in a mirror?" Sometimes the clothes and the color combinations just don't go well together, but usually it is a case where the person has too much body to fit into too little clothing. Almost every Saturday we see obese young women, stuffed so tightly into their spandex pants that they remind me of plump sausages in their casings. Everything is so tight on them that too many parts of their anatomy become, unfortunately, all too clearly visible.

It is also interesting to observe how parents interact with their children. The kids usually come running up to our booth to look at the shiny and colorful products, while the parents stroll up leisurely behind them. Some parents call out to their kids, "Just look with your eyes, don't touch." Then, as the parents come closer, they tell them that they like this bracelet or those earrings, or wouldn't Uncle Steve like that White Sox ornament? It is a joy to work with these kids and their parents. But – you can well imagine what comes next – then there are those parents who either have no control over their children or simply do not care what they do. These kids grab for anything within their reach; they pull the bracelets out of the holders or pull at the baubles, which I had hung so meticulously on their respective racks. These ornaments are delicate objects, and once the top has been pulled out of them, it takes my wife quite some time to get them back into perfect condition. To make matters even worse, these kids often have greasy or sticky hands because they just ate a donut or are in the process of eating a snow cone with the syrup leaking all over the place. We watch them like hawks, and sometimes we have to tell them, "Please don't touch." Most of the time the parents are somewhat embarrassed and tell the kids to stop, but some of them get a little huffy and they say, "Come on, let's go, we have other things to see." And believe me, that suits us just fine.

These Saturday mornings have become an important part of our life. Here we meet old and new friends. We enjoy the hustle and bustle and all the colorful characters that may appear on any given market day. We are ready for anything, because we know that even though you think you have seen it all, there will still be something that will take us by surprise.

And that surprise happened two years ago. When the husband and wife and their son, who had just looked at our merchandise, had moved along, we saw her standing there, a few feet in front of us. She was a tiny person, definitely shorter than five feet. She wore a gray skirt and a dark red jacket. Her tiny feet were in equally tiny black shoes. She stood there motionless looking at us. She stepped up to our table and let her eyes wander across the displays. Every so often, she would look up and look directly into our eyes, and then turn back to our merchandise. Although I couldn't put my finger on it, I knew that there was something very special about this gentle stranger.

She was an exquisite little lady. Her face was angelic and her skin was so delicate and smooth for her age. Her mouth was sweet and her nose was, I don't know what else to call it, "dainty." But her most outstanding feature was her eyes. They were the brightest blue, so lively, quick and twinkling. She stood there for quite a while, moving a step or two to the left and then to the right. She did not touch anything, and did not look at anything else except the Swarovski jewelry. She looked at us again and said, "So beautiful. Thank you." Then she turned and walked away and was soon lost in the crowd that had now filled the market.

She was back two weeks later and came straight to our booth. She looked over our display the same way she did last time and then said, "I'll take these blue earrings, please," and she pointed to a set of lovely light blue crystal ones. My wife took them off the rack, placed them in a small bag and handed them to her. The little lady took out an old-fashioned money purse from her jacket pocket and took out a five-dollar bill and five singles. She looked at both of us again, her eyes sparkling just as last time. She said, "Thank you," gave us a last smile and walked away. Our eyes followed her until she was out of sight.

She came back several more times that year, and each time she bought a pair of earrings or a pendant, the two most inexpensive items among our offerings.

She made her appearance again last year around the middle of June. This time she said, "Hello," as she approached our table and her voice sounded as if she were speaking to old friends. Again, she looked over the earrings and the pendants, and then she asked my wife what was the birthstone for July. My wife told her it was the ruby and showed her a pair of earrings and a pendant to match in that color. The little lady looked from one item to the other, and then at us, and now back to the earrings and the pendant. She looked as if she had a very difficult decision to make, and this about two items that cost ten dollars each. Finally, she pointed to the pendant and said, "They are both so pretty, but I think I'll take the pendant." Again she opened her money purse and this time she did have a ten-dollar bill.

I could not contain my curiosity any longer when, after her fifth visit last year, and with the market season coming to an end, I simply had to know who she was and what she was doing with the jewelry that she bought from us. They certainly could not be for her, because she never wore any jewelry that we could see. My wife thought it was a silly thing for me to do, but I decided to follow her to see where she lived. Maybe then I could learn more about this little woman who intrigued us so much.

When she left our booth, she went directly to the exit and continued to walk along the street that runs parallel to the railroad tracks that run right through the middle of this suburb. She walked a few blocks and then turned right at the street, which leads to the downtown section of this town. I stayed a good distance behind her, but I did not have to fear being discovered, for she never turned around, but walked straight ahead. She continued for another few blocks and then turned left. I hurried my steps so as not to fall too far behind, just in case she should disappear into a building. And that was a good idea, because just as I turned the corner, I saw her go into a building that was slightly more set back from the street than the other buildings. It was an older building, constructed of dark red brick and seemed to be one of those apartment buildings, four to six units, that were built around here back in the fifties and sixties.

Now that I knew where she lived, I went back to the market and told my wife what I had found out about her. She just shook her head and called me "a silly man."

We waited for her to come back this summer, but she did not return. We waited until the end of August, and then I decided to go back to the house where I assumed she lived. Maybe someone there knew something about her. If she was sick, we definitely wanted to send her some flowers and indicate to her that we thought of her and that we missed seeing her.

When I approached the building, I was in for quite a shock. Next to the front entrance was a small, metal sign on which it read, "Queen of Angels – Home for Girls." This obviously was not the building in which she lived. I debated what to do, but then I decided to go inside. Maybe someone in here knew something about her. Upon entering, I was met by a young lady who seemed to be a volunteer at this place. I told her about the little woman who had bought jewelry from us at the market and that I saw her come into this building. The young lady did not know anything about that, but she told me that she would get Sister Agnes, who was in charge of this home. Sister Agnes, dressed in the modern nun's habit, appeared shortly and I began to tell her my story. As I spoke, a smile formed on her face, and before I could finish, she held up her hand and interrupted gently, "I know whom you mean. I saw her here several times last year, but since I was not in charge at that time, I never really paid much attention to her. She must have gotten permission to come in here from Sister Barbara, who was the administrator of this home until she got ill and could no longer fulfill her duties. That is when I was put in charge. I only saw this woman come and go, and I know that she always brought something for the girls, so, of course, I did not object to her visits."

"Does anyone know her name?" I asked.

Sister Agnes thought about this for a few seconds and then said "Come to think of it, I never heard anyone call her by any name. I only know that some of the volunteers would say, 'Here she comes, here comes the little angel.'"

"The little angel" what a perfect name for that gentle, serene, sparkling-eyed woman, who had appeared so quietly into our lives. No one knew where she came from; no one knew where she had gone. She brought joy into the lives of girls who had not experienced much happiness in their fragile lives. She brought joy to us by reminding us that there are people like her out there – the quiet, unseen and unheralded "angels" who make all the difference in the world.

Hundreds of people move past our booth every Saturday; hundreds of people come and go in our lives every day – but it is you, little angel, whom we will remember forever.

TICK, TICK, TICK...

"What the hell am I going to do with this?" was the first thought that went through my mind after I had torn the wrapping paper off the gift box that Manfred had given me for my 70th birthday. The picture on the box showed a clock, an alarm clock, more precisely, a projection alarm clock. I already had an alarm clock, and it was working just fine. I decided that this one could serve as a standby just in case the other one ever gave out on me, so I put it in my closet and forgot all about it.

Well, I didn't forget all about it for too long, because pretty soon thereafter I somehow strained my shoulder muscle and the pain extended all the way up into my neck. I was sure that this would soon pass and gave it no more thought – until I woke up one night and tried to look at my alarm clock, which stands on a dresser to the left of my bed. I turned my head in that direction and a pain shot through my neck, a considerable pain. I got up and moved the dresser a little forward so that I would not have to crane my neck to see the numbers on the clock. The problem now was, since I sleep almost totally flat on my back (this helps my breathing problem) I had to lift up my entire upper body to see the display on the alarm clock. And that motion, the head tilted forward, shot another sharp pain up my neck. It must have taken that sudden jolt of pain that reminded me of the box sitting on the top shelf in my closet. I made up my mind – first thing in the morning, I would set up that contraption to see if that would help me. I went to sleep, chuckling a little to myself – so, it had finally come to this – I needed a two by four smacked across my head in order to realize that I had a remedy for my problem sitting there only a few feet away just waiting to be plugged in. And maybe Manfred's gift wasn't that crazy after all – well, we would soon find out!

The next morning, right after breakfast, I opened the box and took out the clock. The instructions for setting the time and the alarm were very easy to follow and in a few minutes I had the clock up and running. I plugged it in, laid down on the bed, reached up (painfully) and shut off the nightstand lamp. Thinking ahead, I had not opened the blinds this morning. And lo and behold, there it was on the ceiling – 8:42; with two dots between the hour and the minutes blinking on, blinking off, blinking on, and blinking off. I watched this until, what seemed to be a long time later, I suddenly saw 8:43; again with the two dots going on and going off, on and off. Only one more slight adjustment was needed – no problem. I tilted the projection beam just slightly higher onto the ceiling so that the numbers were now almost directly above me. Yes, this was much better – no more twisting the neck sideways or lifting the entire upper body forward. All I had to do was to open my eyes, and there it was, the exact time of day, or actually, of night, displayed clearly right above me.

I forgot about my new alarm clock until that night. As usual, I had read a few pages; this time it was a biography of President Grant (interesting fellow) until that time when I felt my lids getting droopy, and on more than one occasion, the book had actually fallen out of my hands and down right on top of my face. For this reason, I prefer paperbacks – they are not so heavy to hold up, and should that ever happen, that was no big deal. A big and heavy hardcover book, I think it was about Christopher Columbus, once nearly broke my nose when it slipped out of my hands just before I fell asleep.

I shut off the light – and there it was, 10:46; the two dots went on and off, on and off, until the time became 10:47. And the two dots kept on blinking. Suddenly something came into my mind: did those two dots blink at a specific interval, or did they just blink randomly? I decided to find out. When the time switched to 10:48, I counted along with each blink of the dots, and sure enough, at exactly 60, the clock changed to 10:49. So, the blinks occurred at one-second intervals. Now I decided to test how good my sense of time was. When the clock turned 10:50, I closed my eyes and counted to myself. At 59, I stopped and opened my eyes, but the clock was already showing 10:51. I had obviously counted too slowly. At 10:52, I tried it again. This time, when I opened my eyes at 60, the clock was still at 10:52, and blinked five more times before it switched to 10:53. My count had been five seconds too fast. This fascinated me. Somehow it became very important to me to time the length of a minute as accurately as possible. With my eyes wide open, I counted along with the blinks of the dots above my head. Then, when I was sure, I had the right rhythm, I closed my eyes again and counted – this time I opened my eyes only two seconds too early. That definitely was an improvement.

I played this game every night before I fell asleep. After a couple of days, my timing was so good that usually I came within one second of being correct, and quite often I hit it right on the head. Then I posed myself another challenge. Could I time two minutes correctly, or what about three minutes? So, after I had become tired of reading, I would shut off the light and wait for a full minute to appear on the ceiling. Now I would close my eyes and begin to count – sometimes to 120, sometimes to 180. I would usually open my eyes a few seconds before I thought the correct time had arrived. If I did not do this, then, if I opened my eyes too late, I would have to count along to the next minute to see by how many seconds I was too late. I needed to know this to determine by how much I had to adjust my counting rate.

I played this game for several weeks and I was getting quite good at it. I usually came within just a few seconds, even with longer time spans, such as three or five minutes. But in a way, it was also getting tedious. I had to find a way to make this more interesting. Suddenly, I had an idea. That evening, before going to sleep, I had listened to music - not just any music, mind you - classical music, to be more precise, Mozart's "Eine Kleine Nachtmusik," a piece of music that always delights me. And like many other people, I am sure, I can hum the entire first movement in my mind, even without the music playing. So, this is what I did. I went back to my study, found my Mozart CD and looked at the cover. The length of the first movement was five minutes and fifty-two seconds. Then I listened to the piece, sang along and tried to really get the timing down pat. Then I went to bed, waited for a full minute to appear on the ceiling, closed my eyes and "sang" the first movement in my head, carefully observing all accelerando and retards, just as the famous conductor did on the CD. When I opened my eyes, I saw that five minutes and thirty-nine seconds had passed. That meant, that I was off by twelve seconds. I repeated this experiment again on the next night - I listened to the piece, got the tempo into my head, and then laid down, with the light off and "played back" the music in my mind. This time I was off by only seven seconds. I was proud of myself.

I tried this little game with all kinds of variations. For instance, I said the Lord's Prayer out loud and timed it – thirty-eight seconds. Then, on a full minute, I closed my eyes and said it to myself again; this time it took thirty-seven seconds. One second off; that was good. I did the same thing with the National Anthem – one minute and eleven seconds.

Then, when I played this game just before Christmas with Silent Night – fifty-two seconds, I heard a voice, a strange metallic voice. I don't know if it was just inside my head or if it came from somewhere else – this metallic, eerie voice said slowly and very distinctly – "Fool, these are the precious seconds of your life." I had stopped counting the seconds as soon as I heard the first word, "fool." The voice was stern, but also mocking. By the time the phrase was finished in that same non-human voice, my body felt ice-cold even though I was covered from head to toe and had been comfortably warm until that moment when I heard the voice.

"Fool, those are the precious seconds of your life." My heart raced and I felt my body bathed in a cold sweat. Although the voice had sounded so surreal, I could not simply dismiss it as something I had just imagined. That voice, so creepy and piercing, had been real, no doubt about it. I turned the light back on and stared at the ceiling.

I don't know how long I had lain there with my eyes wide open fixed at the ceiling. I had lost all sense of time and had no sense of my surroundings. It must have been quite some time, because when I finally got up slowly and opened the blinds, I saw that first glimmer of sunlight in the east – it was five minutes after five. I know that I had read until midnight; after that, I had played my "game" for a little while. That means that I must have lain there, staring at the ceiling somewhere around four hours. That would not have happened if all of that had just been a dream; if it had been something that just slipped through my mind or a phrase that I might have heard in a song or in a movie and which just came back to me at just that moment. I stood at the window for a long time and watched as the red strip on the horizon grew wider and wider.

Needless to say, I packed that clock away later that morning. I no longer have an alarm clock in my bedroom; instead, I put my wristwatch on the nightstand, but I hardly ever look at it. I fall asleep when my eyes are too tired from reading and I wake up, well, whenever I wake up. But several times a day, regardless of what I am doing, the voice appears, as eerie as ever and it says in its serious, yet mocking tone, "Fool, these are the precious seconds of your life." And I agree, these are the precious seconds of my life, and even though I no longer have an alarm clock, and even though I hardly ever look at my watch, I feel them ticking away, steady and inexorably, on and off, on and off, tick, tick, tick, tick....

CALL ME HANK

Some things make me mad. I mean really mad. Like that friggin' kid from across the street who keeps throwing sticks at the squirrels burying their winter supply of food between the bushes on his front lawn; or that jerk at the end of the block. He puts poison in his back yard to kill stray cats that might be wandering around the neighborhood. He thinks nobody knows about that, but I do. Yessiree, I do!

Why am I telling you this? Well, let me start at the beginning. My name is Hank. At least I'll tell you my name is Hank, but you really don't have to know my name. It don't matter. You like that – "it don't matter?" Even better I think is "it don't matter none." Some people actually talk like this. That cracks me up!

So, where was I? Yep, call me Hank. I live in a quiet mid-western town, not too far from a big city. Sometimes I take the train downtown and wander around a bit. I still don't understand why everybody wants to be here at the same time. It's so crowded. You have to be careful that you don't step on somebody's heels. I did that once, and boy, did that lady give me a dirty look. I felt like telling her, why don't you watch where you're going. But before I could say anything, she called me a jerk, and moved on huffing and puffing with that big, fat behind of hers.

Yes, I live in a quiet little town, actually a suburb of that big city, which I will not name. I live in the basement of a nice two-story house, a house my parents left me when they died. The house is all paid for, and the rent that the two families pay is enough to cover my modest living expenses. The tenants are all right. The couple on the first floor is Macedonian. Macedonian, not Greek, I was told quite emphatically by the old man - as if I knew the damned difference. An old lady lives with them. Always dressed in black with a black scarf over her head - kind of creepy, if you ask me.

On the second floor is an old hippie couple. He keeps an ancient Harley in the garage, but he never rides it. His hair is tied in a long gray ponytail. Freaks me out. His old lady - that's probably what he calls her - is tall and skinny and always wears tight jeans and an old T-shirt - no bra, I'm embarrassed to say.

Just went over the stuff I've told you so far. I'm kind of rambling, I know. By now you've probably guessed that I'm not much of a writer. But before I go on, I've got to go back to the beginning - that line about getting mad. I don't like it when people swear in public, and especially if they swear in front of little kids. About three weeks ago, down at the K-Mart, there was a woman who was really having a hard time with her kid. The boy was maybe three years old. She jerked him around by his hand, bent down and poked a finger in his face. A little while later I heard her tell the kid, "Shut your goddamn mouth or else." That's not right. The kid began to cry. She pushed him forward so that he almost fell. I told you I live in a little town. I know where this woman lives. I'm sure she was not so happy when she saw the right rear tire of her car the next morning in her driveway. If she ever does that again, I'll really have to teach her a lesson.

What I also don't like is the way people use the words love and hate. I just looooove those shoes. Don't you just loooooove this outfit? I loooooove these earrings. He really looooooves that book I gave him. I'm not one of those language experts (I can't think of what they're called) but doesn't love require some feeling toward something, like toward another person, or toward an animal, or any living thing? So what kind of a person are you if you loooooove shoes? The same goes for the word hate. I haaaaate the weather here in the winter. I haaaaaate loud music. I haaaaate big gas guzzling cars. How can you hate things, plain ordinary lifeless things? And why be so mean and aggressive? Can't you say I dislike this or that or that is not cool? That is why so many people are so crazy – they looooove and haaaate everything. And then their actions are overblown and weird things happen. Calm down folks; show your love for people and animals that you care about, who never did anyone any harm. I mean, I'm no genius, but doesn't that make sense?

I had good parents. My mother was always loving and kind. My father didn't beat me very much, only sometimes when he thought I deserved it. Here's an example. When I came home from school with my report card, I had an F in algebra. My father called me a lazy bum and beat me. It really didn't hurt much, with me being in high school already and all that. I was really too big to be beaten, but I still think he was wrong. Algebra is a form of math, right? As far as I'm concerned, math is about numbers. You add, subtract, multiply and divide. Period. That's it. Now, our teacher, Mr. Whispers (we always whispered when we spoke about him) brought in these x's and y's and put one thing over another and put parentheses around some numbers and not around other numbers. That got me teed off. This was a math class, so why was he bringing in letters and stuff like that? I asked him once why we had to learn that – it made no sense – and what could you use that for anyway? Those x's and y's wouldn't help you figure out how much money you would get back if you bought something for $7.37, and you handed the lady at the cash register a ten dollar bill. When I think back, I have to say that Mr. Whispers was a patient man, but I still didn't like him very much.

I told you I live in the basement of my house. I like it down here. In the summer, it's nice and cool, and in the winter I don't have to heat too much. Saves me money. Now, I don't live here by myself.

I have some friends who share my living quarters with me. Go ahead, call me crazy, but to me, they are the best friends I ever had.

First, there are my two cats, Sam and Ferdinand. Sam is actually a female, but with that face, I just had to call her Sam. They are both very well behaved. They eat almost anything and are very good about using their litter boxes. Ferdinand always sleeps at the foot of my bed. I have to be careful not to kick him during the night. Sam likes to sleep on my head. Yes, that's right, on top of my head. Sometimes I have to change my position just so I can breathe.

I also have a fish tank. There are fourteen fish in this tank – all cheap fish. I can't afford those fancy ones. They die so quickly. I always have to get new ones. I tried giving all of them names, but I gave up on that. Too many new ones all the time, and the way they swim around, I can't keep up with them. Then there is Speedy, the turtle. Speedy – good name for a turtle, don't you think?

Last, but not least, there is Redeye. He's my favorite. Redeye is a white rabbit with red eyes. What else could I call him? One day he was in my backyard. He just sat there nibbling on the grass. I brought him inside. I went around the neighborhood and asked if anyone had lost a white rabbit. He was obviously somebody's pet, but nobody knew anything about a missing rabbit. So, I kept him.

Redeye is something else, I tell you. He's very quiet and most of the time he minds his own business. Sometimes, though, he rubs against my leg when I'm eating. Then I throw something down to him, and he always eats it, regardless what it is. He really likes donuts – now that's something, isn't it? A rabbit that likes donuts.

He and I always play this little game. When I hold a lettuce leaf out to him, I ask him, do you want some lettuce? He looks at me for a while and then nods his head ever so slightly. Then I ask him, do you really want this lettuce? He looks at me again, and then he nods twice. No kidding. He nods two times. Then I give him the lettuce, but he cracks me up every time he does this. I don't have a dog right now and I don't think I'll get another one. My poor old Suzy, she was sixteen, so gentle and loving, died in my arms. She never complained, just looked at me with those big brown eyes. I petted her for hours and told her not to be afraid, that everything would be all right. Then she stopped breathing.

I like dogs a lot and that is why I'm not sorry for what I did to Mr. Bevin's shed. This a-hole of a man used to beat his dog for no reason at all. Every time he got angry, he beat him. Finally, I couldn't take it any longer. When he left on vacation (with his dog), I snuck into his backyard one night and started a little fire by the side of his shed where he keeps his wood for the fireplace. Nice and dry. I was already back in bed when I heard the sirens. I went past the house the next day and saw that one

110

wall of the shed had some pretty good fire damage. You're lucky this time, I thought to myself. Next time might be a little more serious.

I forgot to tell you why I'm writing all of this down. It's because of the birds - yep, the birds. You see, a couple of weeks ago I went to my mailbox to see whether I got my Pizza Hut coupons. When I get those, I always go down to the Pizza Hut and get myself a sausage, mushroom and onion pizza. Can't beat the price. The large pizza is just right for two meals. These coupons usually come on Fridays and most of the time that's the only mail I get, except, of course, for my utility bills.

So, as I walked across the grass toward my mailbox, I saw a turtle dove sitting right in my path. She did not move until I was about five feet from her. Then she flew away. No, that's wrong. She did not fly. She actually kind of fluttered away, half running, half flying, as if she had a broken wing or something. I think that's the way they try to get your attention away from their nest where the babies are. And sure enough, right in front of me I saw a little bundle of gray feathers. When I looked closer, I saw two tiny turtle dove babies lying in the grass. They must have fallen out of their nest in the red maple tree. I carefully stepped around them to check the mailbox. No Pizza Hut coupons.

I started watching the birds from my basement window. I saw the mother very clearly as she sat quietly on top of her chicks. She sat there again the next morning. Now I began to wonder what she did for food. She never left her babies. The grass around her was yellow and dry. That meant that there were no worms that she could get at.

She still had not moved the following day. She was obviously afraid to leave her babies unprotected on the ground. I got an idea. I had plenty of birdseed in my garage, which I use to fill up the three birdfeeders in my backyard. I just love it when my backyard is filled with birds. There are always plenty of sparrows around, but I also get woodpeckers, hummingbirds and even Mr. and Mrs. Cardinal drop by occasionally. And squirrels, you wouldn't believe the squirrels. They usually eat the seeds that have fallen to the ground, but sometimes they make it up the poles and eat hanging upside down from the feeders. I used to chase them away, but I don't do that anymore. They have to fatten up for the winter, too, because, boy, it sure gets cold around here and they won't find anything to eat then. I do have enough food for all of them.

I got a big scoop full of birdseed and slowly approached the birds. I hoped I could get close enough to pour out the seeds without the mother flying away, so close that she could get at the birdseed without having to leave her babies. Well, that did not work. When I was just about to gently pour out the seeds in front of her, she scattered away, again pretending to have a broken wing or leg or something like that. I poured the seeds right next to the babies who didn't seem to notice me at all.

The next day I brought more food and I was happy to see that most of the seeds had been eaten. Again, I watched from my basement window. The mother just sat on her babies all the time. Then another worry occurred to me. It had not rained. They had to be getting thirsty. I thought about bringing out a saucer filled with water, but I gave up on that idea. How could the mother get the water to her babies? They would still be thirsty. A saucer in the grass would just attract everyone's attention when they walked by on the sidewalk. I didn't want that to happen. Then it hit me. Worms! They had to have worms! That way they would get the vitamins, carbo something or other, or protein that they needed. And worms are juicy, right? So I started to dig in my yard, but guess what. The soil was so dry that I dug and dug and couldn't find any friggin' worms. Now, I hope you don't think that the word "friggin" is swearing; but I got so mad that I actually said out loud, "Where are you, you friggin' worms?" I was mad and I hear a lot of people talking a lot worse than that. So, pardon my French, if you are offended.

Boy, this writing stuff sure is hard. After about an hour, I get a headache. You probably noticed that all of this is in short sections. That's all about what I can write at one time.

Now, back to the worms. I didn't find any. There was only one solution. I had to buy them. Luckily, the J and B Bait Shop is not all that far away from my house. So I got on my bike and rode over there. I bought two plastic containers full of fat, juicy worms. They call them night crawlers. Keep them in the refrigerator, the man told me. I paid five dollars and fifty cents for the two containers – about the price of my pizza.

When I came home, I took out two worms and carried them out to the birds. The mother hobbled away again. I put the two worms right in front of the two baby birds. They actually looked at me. Later, I noticed that the mother was pecking away at something. It had to be the worms. After a while, I went out again with two more worms. I saw that the first two were gone. The grass was so dry that the worms couldn't have dug themselves into the ground or could have crawled away. The mother found them and fed them to her babies. I hope she had some herself. This made me happy.

I did the same thing for the next three days. I always brought out birdseed and two worms. There was always less birdseed and the worms were gone. The babies looked a lot bigger. On the fourth day, I woke up with a jolt. Oh, my God! Today the Mexicans would come. You see, ever since I fell off a ladder when I tried to rescue a kitten that had somehow gotten on my garage roof, my back just hasn't been right. And even cutting grass with a power lawn mower is too much for me. My back hurts for days afterwards. So I did what most of my neighbors do. I asked a Mexican crew to cut my grass, too. And they sure do a great job. Four guys; two with those huge lawn mowers, one with an edger and one with a leaf blower. Fifteen minutes and the job is done. Just one problem – they work so fast that they wouldn't notice the mother turtledove limping away when they approached. They would probably mow right over her babies. The thought of those powerful spinning blades chopping up the two little birds, with their mother hovering helplessly a little distance away, almost made me sick – I mean, really sick! I saw that picture so clearly that I almost had to barf. I got to stop now!

I found a few poles in my garage, each about two feet long, and roped off the area around my little invalids. Guess what happened? The Mexicans never came. It had been so dry that the grass hadn't grown at all and it didn't need to be cut. I did, however, leave the ropes up just in case they decided to come another day. But they didn't.

This went on for another five days. I would feed the birds three times a day. Each time, I noticed that the worms were gone and that some of the seeds had been eaten. The babies looked a lot bigger, too.

Then, one morning when I went out to feed them, the mother hobbled away as usual, but one of the chicks flew away. Yep, just swooped up and flew away. This made me feel really good! They were clearly ready to make it on their own. And the next morning, when I looked out of my basement window, I saw that the mother was not sitting in her usual place. Something must have happened! I went outside in my pajamas. Yessiree, I saw that all three of them were gone. There were just a few tiny feathers on the ground. No signs of a struggle or fight. They had obviously just flown away. I was so happy! They had made it! I felt good! I didn't care what that crazy old Mrs. Gardner thought, (oh, yes, I saw her peeking out from behind her curtains). I had done my job. Missions accomplished! That afternoon I went to Pizza Hut and ate my pizza with sausage, mushrooms and onions, even though those goofballs never did send me my half-off coupon.

Well, that's my story. You probably think I'm a little nuts caring so much for animals. You think I'm just a big softie, right? Maybe you think of me as just a goofy wimp getting all teary-eyed when I see any kind of suffering – especially children and animals. Well, if that's what you think, that's all right with me.

Now, at the beginning I told you that some things make me mad. No, it's not things that make me mad. It's people that get me mad – really mad sometimes. And sometimes I do something about it. I gave you two examples in this story, but there were more, quite a few more. As far as I'm concerned, they had it coming.

So, listen here. If you should ever think about hurting a child or an animal, or if you ever abuse any living thing – watch out! I might be right behind you, and I'll find out where you live, and then....

Ha, ha, ha, just kidding!

And maybe NOT!

ABOUT THE AUTHOR, HELMUT STEFAN

Helmut Stefan is a retired Chicago public school teacher who loves to travel, read and write.

In 1998 he was awarded a National Endowment for the Humanities Fellowship to study "Mozart, the Man, his Music and his Vienna." Classical music, especially the music of W. A. Mozart, is one of the great passions of his life.

He and his wife Ingrid and their grown children live in the Chicago area.

Other books by Helmut Stefan:

Trio in D minor

Feathers in the Wind- short stories

The FBC –The Full Bladder Club. One man's encounter with nine weeks of external radiation therapy for prostate cancer. A story about an adult disease told with an adult sense of humor.

www.ingramcontent.com/pod-product-compliance
Lightning Source LLC
Chambersburg PA
CBHW071133250626
47159CB00006B/2223